Erebus

Ten Stories

Yen-Kheng Lim

and

May-Han Thong

*Sri*Books

Singapore

Erebus: Ten Stories

Published by SRI Books,
An Imprint of the Simplicity Research Institute,
Singapore.
www.simplicitysg.net
enquiry@simplicitysg.net

Artwork by May-Han Thong

Disclaimer:
This is a work of fiction. Other than the well-known per-
sonalities and literary characters mentioned incidentally
in some chapters (which we gratefully acknowledge), the
rest of the characters in this book and the events surrounding them are the product of the authors' imagination: any resemblance of the latter to actual persons or
events is purely coincidental.

A CIP record for this book is available from the
National Library Board, Singapore.

Edition SRI-2016-5

ISBN: 978-981-11-1762-6 (p-book)
ISBN: 978-981-11-1763-3 (e-book)

May Han:
To Miss Mumtaz, who told me I should write.

Yen Kheng:
To my Mum, Dad and Sis.

Acknowledgements

MH: I would like to thank my family, especially my long-suffering father, who read and reviewed everything I wrote from my teenage years until now without complaint. I write *a lot,* so this is no easy feat. Thank you, daddy, for supporting my dreams even though you were busy paying bills. Special thanks go to my collaborator YK for going on this mission with me. I was just joking when I said I would drop-kick you if you refused, but I must have looked more serious than I intended to. I hope you had fun writing at least.

YK: Thanks to MH for working on the book with me, and for not drop-kicking me. (I would have preferred the roundhouse kick instead.)

We are equally grateful to Dr. Cindy Ng, Tao Ye, Naz, Huay Lian, Ethan, and the whole army of friends, relatives, friends of relatives, and relatives of friends, for reading the first drafts and giving us valuable feedback and ideas to make our stories better.

We are also thankful to our publisher, SRI Books, and to Dr. Rajesh Parwani, for helpful comments and assistance during the editing and production process.

YK & MH

Planet Earth
November 2016

Contents

Ερεβος (Greek)

Erebus (Latin)

"deep darkness, shadow"

Source: Wikipedia
www.wikipedia.org

UNDER STARLIGHT

YK

I

'Kathy, look!' said the father to his 12-year-old daughter.

Kathy slid across the backseat of the car towards the window and looked out into the darkness. They were on an open country road with no street lights. It was pitch black.

'Look at what?'

'Look up,' he said, 'at the stars!'

Kathy did, and her mouth opened in amazement as she looked at the sparkling assortment of lights sprinkled across the sky.

She continued looking quietly as her father pulled the car over to the side of the road.

'Why are you stopping?' Mum protested, 'We're already late as it is.'

'It'll just be a few minutes,' said Dad, 'come on Kathy, let's have a better look.'

They got out of the car, leaving the engine running with her mother inside. Kathy and her father took a few steps on the damp ground away from the car.

'Eleanor, could you turn off the lights?' said her father. Soon the headlights went off, and everything was even darker than before. As Kathy's eyes took a moment to adjust, her remaining senses seemed to fill the gap. She could smell the distinct petrichor mixed with the exhaust from their old, inefficient car engine. The cold, damp grass spilled over the base of her sandals and touched the sides of her feet. Almost immediately, she stopped noticing the smell or the wet grass as she saw the most dazzling show of lights the sky could only offer on the clearest of nights.

'Beautiful, isn't it?' said her father.

'Yeah,' was the only response Kathy could manage, as she looked at the various twinkling stars. She pointed at one and asked her father if he knew its name.

'I don't know that one,' he said as he turned to face west, 'but look at those three up there.'

She stepped closer next to him to see where he was pointing. 'The three stars almost in a row?'

'Yes! That's Orion's belt.'

'So, that must be the Orion constellation then,' said Kathy.

'Can you find a star that's has a different colour than the rest?'

'On Orion? They all look the same to me.'

'There's one that's a bit redder than the rest...'

'Oh yes! That one! On the bottom left.'

'That's Betelgeuse,' said her dad, 'it has that colour because it's a red giant. It's very old and near the end of its life. So, the star just balloons up and turns red. It's thousands of times larger than our sun!'

'You mean it's about to explode?' Kathy frowned.

'Soon, like probably a few thousand years from now.'

She admired Betelgeuse for a moment longer, when her father said, 'so those three stars which make Orion's belt, do you see how they almost sit on a straight line?'

'Yeah...?'

Kathy's dad stretched his arm forward, pointing at the stars. 'Follow that line straight down. Do you see that star? It's exceptionally bright.'

'Yes! I see it!'

'It's called Sirius. It's the brightest star in the sky.'

'Is it the brightest star in the universe?' Kathy asked.

'No, it's bright to us because it's extremely hot and it's quite close to where we are.'

As her dad was explaining this, her mother called out from the car, protesting that her sister was waiting for them, and might worry. So, they started back towards the car.

'How do you know about all this, Dad?'

'I read it in a book.'

'Okay, so how do people know all these things about the stars in the first place?'

'Well, people have been observing the sky for many hundreds of years. Today, it's a science called astronomy. It's the astronomer's job to study them and understand things about them.'

'Why?'

'They are scientists. They seek to understand as much as they can about the world around us.'

'So, astronomers spend their nights looking at the stars?'

'I suppose so... they use telescopes.'

'I think I want to be an astronomer when I grow up.'

'I thought you wanted to be an astronaut?'

'I know someone like me could never be an astronaut,' Kathy grinned as she looked around the vast expanse of the sky, 'but I also know I would never get sick of looking at a view like this for the rest of my life.

II

With no small tinge of envy, Kathy looked at Cynthia, whose head was resting on Josh's lap further down the beach. She could hear their faint murmur of conversation, but could not make out the words as they were drowned out by the sound of waves lapping against the sand.

For the longest time in secondary school, Kathy had a crush on Josh. She had seen Josh's girlfriends come and go, and as each one left, she had hoped for the chance to befriend him, but no such opportunity came. She thought that night at the beach would be her last chance. They had finished secondary school and A-levels, and each of them would be going their separate ways to different colleges and universities. Cynthia and Kathy had planned to celebrate the end of an era with a bang; an epic all-night party at the beach. But it was barely 1 am, and most of the other friends had left. What was once the barbeque fire was now dying embers of red charcoal. Somehow Cynthia and Josh hit it off and were now talking quietly alone down the beach.

Richard and Ed were the two other guys who were still around. Kathy did not know them well. Heck, the only person who Kathy knew there had her head resting on her long-time crush. So, Kathy sat alone in the sand, knees up to her chin, smelling of grease and smoke and wondering why she chose to stay until dawn. Well, it was clear why she chose to stay, and she regretted that decision now. She stared at the blackness of the sea, thinking that her future looked exactly like that now. Where you know that there must be plenty of stuff happening beyond, just that you can't see any of it at the moment.

Kathy noticed that Richard and Ed seemed to have gone quiet. A short while ago they were chasing crabs all around the beach, hooting and laughing. Now it appeared that Ed was trying to convince Richard to do something, gently nudging his shoulder. Richard seemed hesitant and embarrassed. Kathy lost interest in them and turned her attention back to the sea.

She ignored Cynthia and Josh's faint conversation, as she focused on the sound of the waves. She found it soothing and closed her eyes to shut everything else out, enjoying the peace.

In the past few months, her head had filled with what she called 'white noise'.

It was her shorthand for uncertainty. Not knowing what her A-level results would be like. Not knowing which university to apply to. Not knowing which ones would accept her. Not knowing if she could afford the tuition fees. Not knowing if Josh would figure into any of this — that one was a long shot, she admitted to herself.

When things are uncertain, you naturally think of all the possible outcomes and try to plan, or imagine how each of them would pan out. But the less you know, the harder it is to think of possibilities. And in trying to see what your future would be like, all you end up with is an unresolved blizzard of snow from an out-of-tune television — white noise. So, for months, Kathy had been crushed under the weight of her future, while her present continued to push her up against it.

Some clarity and certainty came when she got accepted into a university under a modest scholarship. But she knew that soon her life would be thrown into chaos all over again as she tried to adjust to her new routine and surroundings. For now though, this very night at the beach, she could just tune everything out. It was a chance to enjoy a moment of serenity. She wished she had her MP3 player with her. This was the perfect atmosphere to listen to Zero 7, or maybe the slower songs from Pearl Jam. But the sounds of Nature were soothing too, as she listened with her eyes closed and —

'Beautiful night, isn't it?' said Richard, startling Kathy out of her reverie as he sat down on the sand, uninvited.

'Ya,' said Kathy.

'Look, Orion is bright and clear tonight,' he said.

Right then, it occurred to Kathy that she hadn't looked at the stars since her father died last year. Because astronomy was her father's hobby, seeing anything related to space and the stars just reminded her of him, and it always made her sad.

'I guess it is.'

'Isn't it amazing, the light from the stars coming to us from many years ago? We're seeing into the past!'

'Yup, the speed of light is finite,' said Kathy.

'And universal. Strangely, time isn't.'

Kathy glanced side-eyed at him.

'Time is different for different observers. We always assume that time is like the same for everyone, on the same straight road that stretches to eternity. But it isn't.'

'Richard, I've seen that movie.'

'What movie?'

'The one where Benedict Cumberbatch plays Stephen Hawking, where you just stole those lines from.'

'Hah!'

'If you want to mansplain to me,' said Kathy, 'at least be original.'

After a brief pause, he said, 'I still think the night sky looks amazing,'

'It does,' Kathy agreed.

'Why, though?'

'I have no idea.'

'I mean, isn't it strange? We humans evolved to be attracted to things that help us survive, right? That's natural selection. I mean, when we say someone is "beautiful", in terms of biology, that person is fit and can provide healthy offspring, right?'

'I guess.'

'But why would we evolve to find the sky so beautiful?'

The conversation fizzled out fast, and soon Richard was back with Ed, leaving Kathy alone with her thoughts. She tried focusing on the sound of the waves again, but this time her eyes remained open, looking up at Betelgeuse, thinking about the time her father stopped the car just to show her the stars. She could feel tears starting to well up in her eyes.

In about two weeks, she would leave for the university to study physics. Kathy chose that because the scholarship was only offered for certain science majors, and physics was what she was good at.

But then, looking at Betelgeuse again, it occurred to her that she should carry on her father's interest in the skies. The apple had not fallen far, and she realised that the stars were as inspiring to her now as when she was twelve. Contemplating the vastness of space put everything in perspective, her father said.

She could just barely make out the faint band of the Milky Way stretching upwards from the horizon. The gargantuan arm of the galaxy curving across the sky like the arms of a pirouetting cosmic ballerina. It made you feel small and insignificant, but at the same time it elevated you.

Richard did have a point. Why do we find the stars so beautiful?

III

Kathy saw stars.

But this time they were the kind you saw under your eyelids after being knocked hard on the head. Speaking of which, she felt like her head was spinning, or was it her body? She wondered.

She slowly unstuck her bloodied face from the deflated air bag.

'Shit,' Kathy said to herself. She was in big trouble now. This wasn't even her car. She had borrowed it from a friend to attend the party. And she had drunk way too much.

'Dammit, Tommy,' she grumbled, still mad at her boyfriend whom she had met in her first year of university.

In the ditch, the car was at an angle. The driver's side was tilted upwards, and out of the window she could see the familiar Hunter holding his eternal pose in the night sky.

'Hello again, Orion,' Kathy slurred. She realised the accident might have sobered her up a little, as the analytical part of her mind seemed to be working, and was now wondering if she'd be in this ditch if she had never met Tommy and Ruth, and how everything had led to this one moment. She was here to study physics, to 'understand you', she said to Orion.

She thought back to her very first class on the first day, on how excited she was to be here. And how every little thing the professor said sounded new and exciting. But she missed home; she had never lived alone before. Though strictly speaking, she was not alone now — there were plenty of people in the dormitory. Still, it was not the same as being at home.

Kathy's best friends at the dorms were Ruth and Tommy. Tommy studied business and Ruth was in engineering. It was surprising that they had anything in common at all. The three of them were in different faculties, came from different countries, but they would spend all night at a 24-hour coffee shop, talking endlessly. When they first met, Kathy was surprised and glad to have met such friendly people. She even wondered why they would be that nice to her, and to each other? Perhaps they were genuinely nice people. Or maybe, unconsciously, that was the way they all coped with the loneliness of being so far from home.

The three of them did everything together, going to classes, homework, going out to town, having meals, participating in clubs. Soon, Kathy and Tommy became a couple.

Not counting those she had in secondary school, Tommy was her first serious relationship. It was the first real one for Tommy too, and it took a lot of stumbling and awkwardness before they got comfortable. And even then, they got into a lot of arguments. Her friends, especially Ruth, kept telling her that arguments were normal for couples. Ruth had a theory that couples that didn't ever argue were doomed to fail since they never cared about each other enough to start any arguments. 'You fight because you care about each other,' Ruth said.

Except that, she wondered if Tommy really did care about her. Looking back at all the arguments they had, Kathy felt that they mostly stemmed from the fact that she had thoughts and opinions he did not agree with.

One evening, they were eating at a McDonald's, and seated right next to them was a family with two very young children. One was a toddler and the other a baby who cried a lot. Kathy was irritated by the noise, and her reaction quickly changed Tommy's mood.

'You don't like kids?' asked Tommy, looking bewildered.

'Not particularly... why?'

'Nothing,' he said.

'Do *you* like kids?' Kathy challenged in return.

'Not really, but that's different.'

'Why?'

'Nothing.'

Kathy tried to make him explain, but Tommy managed to convince her to change the subject.

'Are you mad at me?' she asked.

'No, it's fine.'

It's fine. That almost always meant that things were far from fine and that Tommy wanted to brush the subject aside. Which, in turn, meant that there were unresolved issues. Then there was a matter of how Kathy should react to this. If she just accepted him saying 'it's fine', the unresolved feelings Tommy had would just simmer, and that might lead him to feel she didn't care. On the other hand, if she kept trying to talk about the issue then either Tommy would be irritated by her insistence, or they would explode into an argument. Kathy not only had to guess what Tommy meant, but she also had to anticipate his next response. Maybe Tommy only said 'it's fine' because masculine expectations stopped him from ever discussing feelings and emotions. There were layers of weight and meaning when someone says 'it's fine'.

Admittedly, Kathy was sometimes guilty of the same thing. She realised that she could never find the right words to say what she really meant. Words were too fluid, inconstant. How could she trust them to carry information from one mind to another?

True meanings are always hidden between the lines, with infinite interpretations. The rules unclear.

This was when Kathy started to truly appreciate physics. Everything felt more honest. It was all there in the equations, right in front of you. If you failed to understand them, then it was your fault and yours alone. It was harder, but fairer too. No deception.

It all came to a head at the party. Everyone had been drinking, perhaps much more than they were supposed to. Perhaps not everyone made wise judgements. Maybe Tommy shouldn't have kissed Ruth. Perhaps Ruth shouldn't have reciprocated. Maybe Kathy shouldn't have stormed off in anger when she saw them, though she was perfectly right to do so. But Kathy shouldn't have been driving intoxicated.

So, there she was, with the borrowed car angled up in the ditch, staring up at Orion. The anger and alcohol had exhausted her. She was too tired to do anything. If the car caught fire or blew up, then so be it, she thought. But nothing happened. She just sat there, looking at Orion until someone in a passing car saw her and called the police.

She was arrested, charged with driving while under the influence of alcohol, and lost her scholarship.

IV

In her anger, Kathy squeezed the phone so tightly that, for a moment, she thought it might break.

The email had come from the Graduate Studies Committee. It said that without Professor Deesu's approval, they were unable to accept her thesis. The reason given in the email was: 'Professor Deesu states that the results presented in the thesis are either not original, or not produced solely by the student.'

Bullshit.

Kathy knew exactly what was happening here. Deesu was punishing her because of what she did. Also, especially because of what she *didn't* do. It was late in the evening, and she was walking home alone after having dinner with a friend. Despite the street lamps, she noticed that Orion was high up in the sky.

'You're still there, old friend?' She held out the phone at the Hunter, showing him the email.

'I thought science was supposed to be impartial, free of human bullshit,' she said aloud, not caring if people passing behind her on the bridge thought she was crazy. This whole thing was making her lose her sanity. 'I am working in science now, and there are still scumbags trying to fuck up my life. And you're just standing there, doing nothing. I suppose you're being "impartial" now, huh?'

But suddenly she put away her phone and looked down, remembering that if someone from her university saw her like this, it wouldn't help her case at all.

She had to decide. Quit or find a new advisor. Quitting would mean that she had just wasted the last four years of her life. If she found a new advisor, it might take a couple more years, but she would have her PhD. That's assuming her new advisor didn't turn out to be as bad as Deesu.

She had come too far to quit now, having already struggled through her bachelor's degree by working part-time as a waitress to compensate for the scholarship lost after the accident.

If she could time-travel, she thought, all she would do was to go back four years and punch her younger self for her stupidity. Back then, she had already heard some stories about Deesu from her senior classmates, but ignored them and chose to work with him anyway. He was, after all, the worlds' foremost expert on stellar evolution. He had the contact numbers of Nobel laureates in his hand-phone, and might probably become one himself.

Which was why Kathy was so excited that Prof. Deesu was interested in working with her. He said she had good grades and lots of potential. 'We will do amazing things together,' he said. In hindsight, he probably had different 'things' in mind.

Kathy didn't even realise what was happening at first since it began very slowly and subtly. When they met in his office to talk about their projects, he would say that her hair looked great, or that she looked beautiful in that shirt. At first, she just thanked him politely. Usually, she didn't care if people complimented her on her looks, and she thought that was what most guys thought they should do anyway.

But the comments kept getting more specific and un-comfortable. 'I bet you look amazing in a bikini,' he once said. 'Usually, I don't have the energy for this, but having a hot girl like you in the room just gives me a boost,' he said after they had spent nearly two hours working on a prob-lem.

He would put his hand on her shoulder while they worked, or around her waist as they walked together at a conference, all the while admitting that he was a very 'touchy person'. Strangely, when he was around his male students, he was not at all 'touchy'.

The email was sent late at night, but Kathy happened to be awake and saw it. 'Maybe it's the alcohol talking right now,' he wrote, 'but since we've started working together I can't stop thinking about you. I know I could lose my job over this, but I'm insanely attracted to you.'

The email went on and on about how much he wanted to be with her, about how she was an amazing person and a talented scientist. Kathy felt scared after reading it, and her heart was noticeably beating hard and fast. The attraction was not mutual. She was going to have to figure out a way to let him down gently so that they could continue working together.

The next morning, she was glad that Professor Deesu acted like nothing had happened. He came to look for her in the graduate students' room to talk about a minor admin detail, and that was it. She thought everything would go back to normal then.

But the comments about her looks, and the touching, continued. Somehow, almost every conversation with him veered into sexual topics. He talked about the things he and his ex-wife used to do in bed, and how he once had an affair with a graduate student. He asked her personal questions that were way too weird, like, 'Have you ever had sex in public?'

One or two incidents like these in isolation might have been nothing, but because of Deesu's 'supervising style' of working closely with his students, he had plenty of opportunities to make those unwanted advances on her. Over the years, they took a toll on Kathy. She couldn't focus on her work anymore.

When she tried to broach the matter with the other professors, they weren't helpful, most of them saying things like 'yeah, that's Prof. Deesu,' or 'he's just being friendly.'

One evening, when she was alone in the graduate students' room, he found her working there and said that an attractive girl like her should be out partying on a Friday night.

'I don't like partying,' she replied.

'Well, I guess as your advisor I should be happy that you're so hard-working. I have a bottle of champagne in my office. Shall we have our own little party?'

'No thanks. Like I said, I don't like parties.'

'Suit yourself. What are you working on anyway?'

'The analytical expression of the generalised Chandrasekhar limit. It doesn't fit the numerical integration.'

They discussed the Chandrasekhar limit for a while. Until suddenly, during a pause in their conversation, he said, 'Thanks for pretending that I never sent you that email —'

'Which email? We sent each other tonnes of emails,' said Kathy.

'You know which one,' he put his hand on her arm, 'I meant everything I said, though.'

'Please, Prof. Deesu —'

'Come on, don't call me that,' he said, 'let me kiss you.'

He held her arm as he leaned in to kiss her. As she tried to push him away, gently at first, she panicked as she realised how strongly his hand was gripping her arm. When she managed to wrench herself free, she grabbed her bag and went straight out the door.

She didn't set foot on the campus for the next few days, during which time she was trying to decide whether to lodge a formal complaint with the Office of Student Affairs. She eventually did, and they interviewed her. She told them everything that she could. She showed them the email he sent, and described the assault at the graduate students' room. At the end of the interview, they told her not to discuss the matter with anyone else while they investigated the issue.

Since then, she never heard anything from the office. She still hadn't been to the campus at all, just to avoid Prof. Deesu. Until one day she got an email from him, apologising about what happened that day, that he was having a tough time in his divorce, and other excuses. He also wrote that he wished she hadn't filed that complaint with the OSA over this 'misunderstanding' and that she was 'making a big deal out of nothing.'

Kathy finally managed to get an update from the OSA when she went to ask them. They said that the investigation had been completed, and they found that the incident was due to an 'unfortunate misunderstanding'. They stressed that the issue was strictly confidential and that she was not to discuss the case with anyone else, especially the press. Any 'misinformation' would be unhelpful to all concerned, and detrimental to the university's reputation.

Reputation.

That's all universities cared about. Kathy was not surprised. One good thing to come out of this was that Deesu stopped making advances towards her. No more friendly 'chats' about his personal sex life, nor any more questions about hers. But this wasn't because he had learned his lesson — it was because, in his eyes, she was now the enemy.

Kathy found out that Deesu told another professor that she had tried to seduce him, and how she tried to use sexual favours to finish her thesis easily. That professor was the advisor of her friend, who told her about it.

On those days that she did show up on campus, she couldn't tell if she was getting weird looks from people, or if it was all in her head. When she gave talks and presentations, she kept getting challenged about her results and calculations. Everyone seemed to be doubting her research, even though she came fully prepared and could answer all the questions thrown at her.

'It's all your fault,' Kathy said to Orion, more quietly this time. At least there was no one at the bridge at that moment.

'You're the reason I chose this life.' Kathy used to think that all human quarrels were petty compared to the beauty and vastness of space. Her father used to say that if you really looked at the stars, took in the universe, all your earthly problems would shrink into trivial specks floating unnoticed among the galaxies.

'I don't have the same privilege as you, Dad. Either that, or it's a lie.'

V

'Dr. Huang, may I go to the bathroom?' a student asked Kathy.

'Yes, but we'll start soon,' Kathy replied. The kid dashed off the field.

Kathy was a post-doc now, and her research group was hosting a bunch of kids from an astronomical club of a nearby school. She still couldn't believe how she had managed to get this far in physics, surviving all the way through her doctorate. She had quit working for Professor Deesu and moved to another university. It had taken her three more years to finally get her PhD.

All her friends talked about getting new jobs, buying new houses, starting new families. But Kathy's life had none of that, no sense of moving forward or newness. She didn't have a long or serious relationship after Tommy, nor did she want to.

Kathy raised the walkie-talkie to talk to the janitor in charge of the field maintenance. 'Mr. Scott, we're ready for the lights now.'

'Aye, Dr. Huang.'

A moment later, all the lights in the university field were turned off. As everyone's eyes began adjusting to the darkness, she could hear the students murmuring, 'wow'.

'Beautiful,' someone said. The students queued up to take turns looking through the telescope. But Kathy didn't need a telescope at that moment. She saw the Hunter again, bright as ever, holding that eternal, unchanging pose. It's still the same, after all these years. After everything Kathy had been through, she wondered how she could look at the exact same thing and feel differently about it each time.

'Do what you love, and you'll never work a day in your life,' so the saying goes. Twelve-year-old Kathy would have absolutely loved this right now. Looking at the stars for a living. She knew exactly the sequence of nuclear reactions that created the light she was seeing now. She could derive the Friedmann equations that described how the universe expanded. But that saying did not take into account that love doesn't last forever — it didn't with Tommy, after all. And for thirty-four-year-old Kathy, it was now just work.

It was late when the stargazing session ended.

... The Universe Splits ...

Kathy was walking home on a street parallel to the river, occasionally glancing at Orion. She noticed some lights and commotion as she approached the bridge. By the time she reached it, she could see paramedics loading somebody into an ambulance and driving away, sirens blaring. A police officer was also there, questioning witnesses.

Kathy overheard the conversation of a couple of bystanders. Apparently, it was a robbery gone wrong. The guy didn't want to give the robber his wallet, throwing it into the river instead, and got stabbed as a result.

It occurred to Kathy that she now had an answer to a question that was asked sixteen years ago, at the beach.

Why do humans find the night sky so beautiful?

It's because we live in the ugliest place in the universe.

Meanwhile . . .

Kathy was walking home on a street parallel to the river, occasionally glancing at Orion.

Down the street, a man approached. Instinctively, Kathy crossed to the opposite side of the road as she clenched her hand tightly over the straps of her handbag. But when he was close enough for her to see his face, Kathy thought she recognised him.

'Excuse me,' he said, 'you probably don't know me, but I'm a grad student from the university.'

'Yeah, I've seen you around.'

'I just... um...'

'Look,' Kathy interrupted, 'I should be heading home.'

'Right, right,' he seemed apologetic, 'I, uh, just got robbed back there... lost my phone and wallet... I wondered if I could borrow some cab money to get home.'

'What? You should get to a police station and make a report!'

'What's the point? I don't think they would ever find the guy. I'm not good with faces. I won't be able to give a good description.'

His voice was trembling. Kathy could tell that he was still shaken by the incident. Clearly, he wasn't thinking straight.

'Still, you should make a police report about your lost identity card. The robber took it, right?'

'Oh... right.'

'And did you lose any credit cards? You need to call the banks immediately.'

'I don't have a phone.'

'I do. But let's get you to a police station first. It's only a short walk from here.'

Kathy took him to the police station to make the report and lent him her phone so that he could cancel his credit cards. When everything was settled, she gave him her number and went home thoroughly exhausted.

About a week later, Kathy got a call from him. He wanted to take her out to dinner to thank her for her help. She accepted.

At the dinner, she was surprised that she got along really well with him. They had a lot in common and seemed to understand each other's sense of humour. They almost spent the entire night never mentioning the robbery at all, except when they were walking home and she asked, 'What were you doing on the bridge at 1 am, anyway?'

He sighed, and thought for a moment before looking up at the sky, 'I was trying to make sense of my life... the direction it was taking... the stars usually reassure me...'

'...but?' Kathy asked.

'But I got jumped by a guy with a knife.'

Kathy gave a quiet laugh.

'What's so funny?'

'It's weird. I used to look at the stars all the time. My Dad said it helps us keep things in perspective. But it never worked for me.'

'So,' he said, sounding like he was about to change the subject, 'can we do this again, some other time?'

Her mind was screaming loudly, 'yes!' but she just smiled and said softly, 'sure. Call me.'

After they had bid each other goodbye and headed their separate ways, Kathy looked up at the Hunter again. She now knew the answer to the question she was asked at the beach many years ago.

Why do we find the night sky so beautiful?

Because like life, it is mostly bleak and dark, but the bright spots here and there make everything worth it.

THE LOCKED DRAWER

MH

When Zoey heard her father's car start up that Saturday morning, her eyes immediately lost their sleepiness, and she leapt out of bed. 'Daddy!' she yelled, her small feet pattering down the stairs.

'Zoey, I've told you, no running on the stairs!' her mother's stern voice called out.

Those words fell on deaf ears. Zoey ran to her father and wrapped her arms around his legs, partly for shelter from Mommy's impending lecture, but mostly to stall him. 'Daddy, brush my hair before you go!'

Helen sighed. Whoever said that girls were easier to discipline had never met Zoey, particularly when her father was around. 'Daddy needs to go to work now, Zoey. I'll brush your hair later, okay?' she said placatingly.

As usual, Derek had already relented, reaching for the hair brush. 'Helen, it won't take a minute. Anyway, the car is warming up.' He sat down in the living room and placed the ten-year-old on his lap. 'What hairstyle do you want this time?'

'I want a braid! A tight braid, so that it won't come off until lunch time!' Zoey exclaimed.

When Derek drove off to work moments later, Zoey was there at the doorway waving enthusiastically at him, looking pleased with the braid she had requested. She continued to wave until his car turned the corner at the end of the road and went out of sight. By then, she was fully awake, and Helen knew it would be a long day.

As for Zoey, it was to be a very memorable day indeed.

Zoey stuck the pin into the keyhole and pushed it around. She was frowning with concentration, trying to elicit some clicks. There should be clicks, right? In the movies she had watched with her father, when a thief picked a lock with a bobby pin, there were always clicking sounds.

'I'm bored,' Kavin complained.

'Shhh, we're super spies, Kavin. We have to be silent,' Zoey whispered. She twisted the pin, but the drawer remained locked. After a few more minutes of probing and poking, Zoey stomped her foot in frustration. It didn't make sense. In the movies, it looked so easy; a wiggle or two and the lock sprang open.

The child took a step back and stared at the drawer. It had always been locked, as far as she remembered. Her mother had told her that the key was lost, and just like that, the drawer had remained untouched. Zoey had never wanted to know what it contained, until today.

It was just by chance that Zoey got the idea to be a highly trained spy that Saturday. Her mission was to steal an important document inside the drawer. It contained the villain's evil plans, she decided, and it would be up to her to find out what they were. She could not fail; the fate of the world rested in her hands.

'Kavin, get me the metal ruler in Dad's study room,' she commanded. Her little brother jumped off the bed and dashed, returning a minute later with the ruler.

'One way or another, I will unlock this drawer!' With renewed determination, she attacked the lock again, this time wedging the ruler into the slit between the drawer and its frame. Mommy will be so proud of me when I unlock it, she thought. Kavin peered at the keyhole intently, breath held in anticipation.

After a few more minutes, the two children were sprawled on their parents' bed, which, the day before, had been a pirate ship caught in a stormy sea. Their patience was running thin. The lock was being stubborn, and success remained out of grasp. Zoey was beginning to think that being a spy was not that exciting after all. Last week she had been an archaeologist hacking her way through a jungle in search of a lost relic, and for realism she had imagined herself being bitten by mosquitoes. In comparison, even that seemed fun.

'What are we going to do now?' Kavin asked. His dejection was evident.

Zoey pouted sullenly. The locked drawer bothered her. She knew that none of the other drawers or cabinets in her parents' room were locked; her parents were not ones to keep secrets. A short moment of contemplation later, Zoey declared, 'We press on, Kavin. Guard the entrance and make sure the enemies don't get in.'

Once again, she got to work. This time, she got herself another bobby pin and stuck both pins into the keyhole: one at the top and one at the bottom. She wriggled them and thought she felt something giving way.

'Mommy's coming!' Kavin called out urgently.

'The enemy!' Zoey exclaimed. Immediately, she hid the bobby pins in the pocket of her shorts and put the ruler away. By the time their mother got to the top of the stairs, Zoey and Kavin were reading on the bed.

Helen smiled. It was evident that her kids were up to something; they were hardly the kind to lie on their bellies and read on a weekend. Zoey, with her vast imagination, routinely led her brother on some made-up adventure. Reading was as suspicious as it got. 'What are you two up to now?' she asked, placing the neatly folded laundry into the closet.

'It's a secret,' Zoey replied with a big grin. Kavin nodded; Zoey was the leader, after all.

'Alright, but don't get yourself hurt,' Helen said before disappearing through the door. Once she was gone, Kavin returned to his post at the top of the stairway and Zoey's attention returned to the drawer.

This time though, it did not take her long before the lock suddenly gave way. Even Zoey was surprised. With eyes wide with excitement she beckoned to Kavin, and together they pulled the drawer open.

There was a stack of letters, and an old Polaroid camera. Kavin gingerly reached into the drawer and pulled out the camera, and started peering through it. Zoey was intrigued by the letters, bound together with a thin ribbon. 'The documents,' she whispered under her breath. 'I will now know the secrets of the villain!' With a mischievous grin, she clutched the letters to her chest and ran into the room she shared with Kavin.

It took her some time to get used to the cursive handwriting. The papers were yellow with age, and that enhanced her excitement by giving her the impression that the documents were from ancient times. She smoothed out the first letter. It was a short one.

I cried again. It doesn't look like he wants to return to my side. That woman has him wrapped around her fin-

gers, and even for Zoey's sake, he is hesitant. I told him that if he wants a divorce, we're not going to have this baby.

He told me not to be rash. I said Zoey needs a father, but he must never see that woman again. I will not tolerate it. I warned him that if he chooses that woman, he will never see Zoey anymore.

Zoey's heart raced. What is this?

She read the paragraph again, and the realisation came to her: her mother was the writer of the letters. She was stunned; she didn't even know her mother could write. All this while, Helen was hardly known to be very articulate. Zoey was not even sure she had ever seen her mother hold a pen, except to write down recipes or to fill up forms.

Divorce. She knew that word. In movies, when parents divorce, the children must choose who they prefer to stay with. The other parent would go elsewhere, and would only be allowed to visit occasionally. Zoey couldn't bear the thought of not seeing Mommy or Daddy at home; it was always the four of them in the evening, eating dinner together. No, this must be a mistake, she thought. She put the letter aside and began reading the next one.

I discovered that he had been seeing that witch for half a year now. I found her love notes to him, saying disgusting things like, 'I miss you and I wish you were here to rub my back.' How shameless can this woman be? Derek is married with a lovely daughter, and our next child is on the way, and yet she dared to send him this note.

I also found the book she gave him. Derek watched me in silence as I tore it to pieces. I told him I would never give him freedom again. He is to return home immediately after work, every day for the rest of his life. He will not hang out with his friends, or go anywhere without my permission. I will tag along on every trip, and I will read

27

all his letters from now on. Again, he dared not say a word.

A spell of dizziness came over Zoey. Daddy had another woman, and usually in the movies that meant that Daddy was a bad person. Her chest began to heave; the thought of her father, her idol, being anything other than a totally good person distressed her. After all, he bought her books and stuffed bears. He praised her for getting A's, and he kissed her goodnight. He brushed her hair when she woke up, every day without fail. He let her watch adventure movies with him, even when Mommy said those movies were not suitable for little girls. Most importantly, he encouraged her to imagine things. He was the only one who said it was alright for a girl to be a pilot or a race car driver or a soldier. Everyone told her how lucky she was to have a father like hers.

She pressed on with the rest of the letters, which were mostly a repetition of what she had already read. They said the same thing:

He's leaving Zoey and me.

He doesn't love us.

Our marriage is ending.

Zoey supposed she should cry, but there was an overwhelming sense of numbness instead. Mechanically, she stood up. Kavin was still playing with the old camera, but it was only a matter of time before he came seeking her. Slowly, Zoey lifted one corner of her mattress and placed the letters under it.

'Hello, Daddy,' Zoey said as her father bent down to give her a kiss.

Derek did not notice the faraway look in his daughter's eyes as he gave her a hug. 'What did you become today?'

'I was a super spy, Daddy. I stole some secret documents for the government.'

'Oh, really? Did you manage to take down the bad guy?'

Zoey shook her head. 'He got away,' she replied, before skipping away.

Derek smiled, blissfully unaware. That child has a rich imagination, he thought, as he made his way to the dinner table.

It felt like a veil had lifted. For the first time in her life, Zoey saw how her parents really were with each other. She noticed how they never looked at each other when they talked. How her father would hug her and Kavin, but never her mother. She could tell now that Mommy's tone was particularly chilly when she addressed Daddy. They did not even go to bed at the same time; her mother tended to work later into the night, and only retired to bed long after her father was asleep. She recalled how Daddy always bought Mommy expensive gifts for her birthdays and other special dates, but she now saw that Mommy never seemed happy with them.

That night, when Derek kissed Zoey good night, he thought she was particularly stiff. 'Are you okay, Zoey?'

Silently, she nodded. Derek brushed off her strange behaviour as a sign of fatigue from too much playing.

Helen heard the slow, deliberate footsteps down the stairs, and looked up from the sewing machine. Zoey was dragging her feet, and instinctively, she knew something was wrong. 'Zoey?'

'Mommy, I managed to unlock the drawer,' Zoey replied softly.

'Which drawer, honey?'

'The one that you lost the key to.'

Helen jumped, and rushed to the foot of the stairs where Zoey was standing. Her eyes went down to her little girl's hand and saw the letters. With trepidation, she placed a hand on Zoey's shoulder. 'Zoey, did you read them?!' she asked urgently.

In her pyjamas, Zoey looked small and delicate, her confidence and vivacity gone. The letters fell from her hands. Then, the tears came like a deluge. 'I... I wanted to help you, Mommy. I wanted you to be proud and... and praise me for being clever,' Zoey said between sobs.

Helen frantically wiped Zoey's tears off her cheeks, even as her own world turned blurry. She regretted not destroying those letters, but back then, she couldn't. It was killing her, but the best that she could do was to lock them away and throw away the keys. As Derek continued his slumber, all she could do was to try and take the pain away from Zoey.

It was futile. The horrors from the drawer had been unleashed into their home, and she couldn't turn back the clock.

Derek brushed Zoey's hair, carefully sorting out the tangles. 'What are you going to be today, honey?'

There was a long silence. When Zoey finally responded, it was with a shrug and a distant look in her eyes.

REAPER DUTY

YK

Despite what the myths and legends say, I'm not a walking skeleton; nor do I wear a black, hooded cloak. That would be impractical, and very uncomfortable, given the weather these days. Also, I don't carry a scythe. Why would I? I'm not a farmer!

For the most part, I am usually formless. But when I'm on the job, I take the form best suited for the subject. Right now, I have the appearance of a middle-aged woman, dressed in a long skirt and a blouse, with thick glasses. I look like a librarian or someone who works at a public-sector office, someone unassuming, yet carrying an air of authority.

I don't get to choose who I look like for different subjects. All I know is that we will resemble a person that the subject will feel at ease with. Sometimes it's an old fatherly figure, or even a child. Sometimes, I become someone that is close to the subject's age, perhaps someone that reminds the subject of his or her best friend.

But we are not supposed to look like someone the subject knows because we can't speak on that person's behalf — that would be dishonest. And we can't have dishonesty during a Transition. All we need to do is to project an air of familiarity.

I approached the scene, feeling confident. It was my third assignment without supervision, and I was getting the hang of things. I was careful to follow all the tips and advice my colleagues had given me, despite some of them seeming contradictory. This case was a suicide, and I was told that such situations can either be easy or very tricky, depending on the subject.

I was walking amongst tall apartment buildings towards the lights, noise and commotion. The police were keeping onlookers at bay while an ambulance crew approached the body. There was no hurry. The first police officer on the scene had already checked for a pulse. It was too late. Of course; I wouldn't even be there otherwise. Besides, nobody survives a 30-storey fall.

I looked at the body. There he was, a man in his mid-thirties, maybe early forties. From my angle, and with the paramedics surrounding him, I couldn't see his face. So, I took note of the clothes he was wearing: a grey T-shirt and dark pants. I turned away from the scene and looked for someone in a grey T-shirt and dark pants amongst the onlookers. I snaked my way between them to the other side of the street. Of course, I could have walked through them, but then I would have caught a glimpse of their insides, seeing their eyeballs, skulls, or brains. That would have been weird.

Almost immediately I found my subject. Wearing the grey T-shirt and dark pants. He appeared just as he was during his final moments of consciousness. Why is that so? Don't ask me. That's just the way it is. Appearance hardly matters much at this point, since the only ones who could see him were himself and me. He looked serene and calm, almost bored. Half of suicide subjects are usually like that. The other half are the ones who regret the act, so they would either look horrified or be in shock. Not this one, though. He just sat there, looking at his own body through the crowd of onlookers.

I walked towards him.

He noticed me immediately, probably because I was the only one who was not looking at his body that was now being placed into a body bag. We made eye contact, and he looked surprised.

'You can see me?' he asked.

'Yes,' I replied, 'how are you doing?'

He didn't reply. Instead, he just stared at me, wide-eyed.

I began my usual opening line, 'I'm here to —'

'Are you the Grim —'

'My job here is to help,' I said quickly. I hated the name he was about to say. It's offensive. But that's okay since he didn't know any better. Nobody does, until they're in the Transition.

'As I was saying,' I continued, 'I'm here to help you in your Transition.'

He didn't ask what the Transition was. So, I assumed he understood, and I didn't elaborate.

I sat down on the kerb next to him. We both watched in silence as the paramedics placed his body on a stretcher and loaded it into the ambulance.

'Kind of irresponsible for me to go like that. Leaving behind a mess,' he said.

'I suppose you have other thoughts on your mind?'

'I was drunk,' he said, 'should have gone in a cleaner way. I had a method planned. But I was drunk and wanted to get on with it.'

Here's where my real work begins, 'May I ask... why?'

He sat silent for a moment. I waited patiently for him to answer.

'Why not?' he said.

I remained quiet, knowing that he still had more to say.

'As in, why should the default be *not* wanting to go? Even though there's no reason to keep on living?'

'I don't know,' I said, 'seriously, I don't know because I'm not human. But from what I gather, that's what humans do. To keep on going.'

'But I didn't want to go on anymore. That's the point,' he gestured towards the ambulance as it drove away with his body.

'So, there was nothing else in life that you wanted to do?' I asked.

'No,' he replied without hesitation. 'You know how people feel about chores?'

'Are you saying that life is a chore?'

'Something like that, yeah. You get no enjoyment out of doing chores. If it's a chore that you hate, the only way it gets done is by sheer willpower. Forcing yourself to do it.'

'And that's how you felt your life was?'

'Yeah. Every damn thing I did felt like a chore. Getting out of bed, riding my bike to work... and of course, work. Even mundane stuff like putting on my shirt required a huge amount of effort. I couldn't take it anymore. I was too tired. Out of juice. So, I jumped.'

I took notes on my clipboard. 'Why do you think you felt that way?'

'I don't know,' he said, 'I mean, people who knew me wouldn't say I had a hard life. I made a few bad choices — actually, lots of bad choices — and I reached a point where there was no meaning to this life. I had no reason to exist. So why bother?'

'I see.'

'Who are you, anyway? And why do I need help with my Transition?'

'Because these are your final moments. I guess you're fine for the most part because you're a...'

'...a suicide,' he said.

'Yes. But those who die unexpectedly, like in an accident, they might be shocked, and distraught. It is believed that the emotions people feel during the moment of Transition will be locked in eternity.

'"It is believed", you mean you don't know for sure?'

'No. Nobody does. We don't know what happens after the Transition.'

'Wait, if you don't know, then who does? There's gotta be someone who does, right?'

I shrugged. 'How are you feeling now?' I asked.

He considered the question for a moment, then said, 'I feel the same. It seems like nothing has changed. Even though I know that everything just did.'

'Well, while I did say you're mostly fine, but clearly this is the lowest point of your life. Are you sure you want to stay this way forever?'

'It's not up to me, is it?' he asked.

'It is up to you. If you let me help you.'

I stood up and said, 'Let's get out of here. Let's take a walk.'

Quietly, he stood up and followed me.

The streets were quiet now. It was past 2 am on a Wednesday morning, so there weren't many people out and about. We walked together silently for a while. The subject was amused to discover that he could walk through walls and people. That seemed to cheer him up a little. Not that it makes much of a difference, but every little step helps.

'So how is this supposed to work?' he asked.

'It's up to you. First, you need to decide what state you want to be in during the Transition. Perhaps think about something that made you feel contented, or happy about your life. You know when people always say "rest in peace"? Well, we need to find you the peace before you transition.'

'Okay,' he took a deep breath. He seemed to be taking this seriously, which was a good sign. 'I suppose I should recall the time where I felt happy, and think about that?'

'That's a start. What's the most recent memory you have of feeling happy?'

'Well, my company had a promotional booth at a conference a few weeks ago. I was occupying it with a few colleagues. One of them was Catherine. I think that day I felt a connection with her in a way I hadn't felt in a long, long time.'

'I see. Hang on, I can take us there.'

Soon, we found ourselves standing in a nearly empty convention centre. It was a software developers' conference, and it was already over. The centre was closed to the public, and the crew were dismantling the booths and packing the displays.

'There,' said my subject, pointing to a booth. We saw him chatting with Catherine. Both seemed oblivious to the entire conference being dismantled around them.

'I remember that clearly,' he said, 'I enjoyed the conversation so much that I wished it would last forever. I mean, obviously I knew that the crew were taking the entire place apart, and we were supposed to leave, but I wanted to stay on as long as possible. I kept expecting her to say that we should leave, but she didn't. I don't know why.'

'Maybe she wanted to keep talking to you too,' I suggested.

'No way. A disgusting slob like me? No. I would never dare to think that. She was just being polite I guess.'

'But was that your last memory of being happy?' I asked.

'I suppose. I remember thinking, after talking to her for so long, that she understood me. In a way that no one else had before. And I thought I understood her too. There was some kind of shared connection that I couldn't explain. Shit, I don't even know if any of it was real, or if it was just an illusion I conjured up in my mind. Don't I get to find out now that I'm dead?'

Eventually, the crew had to take down his company's displays. They had no choice but to leave. They stood aside for a moment, idly chatting and watching the crew do their work until she said that they probably should go before they got locked inside the centre. They walked out and parted ways as their homes were in different directions.

Then we watched my subject stop on the sidewalk and turn around.

'This is where I thought about asking if she wanted to grab a cup of coffee.'

He stood there, looking nervous at first, then his face fell and I could see his body slouch ever so slightly. He turned around and headed home.

'Guess you never got that coffee,' I said.

'That was the moment I decided that everything in my mind was an illusion after all. There was no connection.'

'So, your last moment of happiness ended on a sad note,' I said. Then I thought about it for a moment, and added, 'But during that isolated moment when you talked to her, were you happy?'

'It was a false happiness,' he said, 'I thought I shared a moment with her, but it wasn't true. How do we even know anything is true? Or if it's just our imagination?'

'It's true if you are willing to accept that not every connection between two people is about romance,' I argued, 'that's not the only way to be intimate. Friends can share deep connections too. Maybe she stayed on talking to you because she felt comfortable, as close friends do. She realised that you were a great person to spend time with. You know, when a woman is friendly with a man, it doesn't mean that she also wants something more. And if a woman only wants friendship with a man, it's not something for the guy to be sad about. Friendships can be special too.'

'Are you telling me not to be depressed that I never got a date with Catherine?' he laughed, 'It's too late now, I already jumped off a building.'

'No, that's not it,' I said, 'I'm telling you to look at this "moment of happiness" that you thought was false and embrace its true value. It doesn't matter that she wasn't interested in a romantic relationship with you. She's still a person who considered you a close friend, and friendship isn't less valuable.'

'I suppose you're right,' he conceded. But I suspect he only said that to stop me from talking. So I suggested that we continue.

Now we found ourselves at the beach. My subject found his past self sitting alone, staring at the setting sun. He had a guitar and a notepad with him.

'This was where I wrote my best songs,' he said, explaining that he once used to be a musician.

'I was sitting there, feeling particularly inspired. All the words and notes just came together in my head. It was beautiful. And when I played it out aloud on my guitar right there, I thought it sounded amazing. It even felt like I was playing a song someone else wrote, because if felt like that song had an existence of its own, and had nothing to do with me.'

I stood silently with my subject, watching himself sitting on the beach furiously writing the lyrics that he had just thought of before he forgot them. Then he played a few bars on the guitar, shook his head, crossed something out on his notepad and wrote something else on it. This went on for a while until he had a complete song. He played it once over in full. It was a simple folk song, and it sounded okay.

'This was one of the few moments where I really felt alive,' he said.

'That song was pretty good.'

'Not good enough to make a living. We didn't get to book enough gigs, and we were always scraping by with very little money. My girlfriend at the time got frustrated and left me. Eventually, I got a job at a software company. So maybe I was happy at that moment, feeling the high of writing a great song. Probably the only time I felt that way. But what's the point if nobody else liked it?'

'I ended up in a job I hated because I couldn't make a living out of doing what I loved. And boy, did I hate that job. I could feel it sucking the essence out of my soul. Coming in during the morning, out in the evening. Turning a crank in an endless corporate machine. My existence was meaningless. Now that I am dead, they have lost a cog which they will easily replace soon enough. And it will go on and on...'

'But the corporate machine is part of the human infrastructure that sustains life so that people can create art in the first place,' I responded, 'If there's no economy, no trade, no stability, or if all we have are wars, then people would be fighting for survival. Then there would be no art. At least you created something,' I said, 'that is part of being human, after all. To create art.'

Next, we were at a time when my subject was seven years old. He was at the dinner table with his mother, talking about what he wanted to be when he grew up. They were going through all the options. The usual, stereotypical ones perhaps. Doctor, lawyer, engineer — but he secretly wanted to be an orchestral conductor. And he asked his mother questions about each job. In the end, he decided that he would be a lawyer if he never got a chance to be an astronaut. Then his mother said that he needed to be a good boy and study hard if he wanted to be a lawyer when he grew up.

Fourteen years later, my subject is in a university. Studying software engineering, not law. But at least that's a career.

Not for long, though.

We were observing my subject getting off the phone after an argument with his mother. He was in his friends' dorm room at college.

'So... what did she say?' his friend asked.

'She said she can't afford my tuition if I lose the scholarship now. So, if I go on the tour, I won't be able to finish my degree.'

'But it's eight cities, man. Thirteen gigs total. There's gonna be at least a thousand people seeing us, at least. That's exposure that most bands will never get in their lifetimes!'

'Yeah, but my scholarship only lasts until the end of this year. I can't finish all the credits by then if we go on the road for five weeks.'

'I know, man. It's a lot to ask. But we can't go without our lead guitarist.'

My subject explained to me, 'So this is where I thought it all started going wrong. In the end, I decided to go on the tour. Never got my degree. But my friend did. He got a job at an IT security firm and quit the band. I was left without a degree or a band. I continued doing it solo, but all I ended up doing was to hop between pubs and bars every night. Singing to drunk and sleepy people.'

But in the midst of performing in dodgy places, every time he sang that song he wrote on the beach, he seemed to forget the entire world around him. He put his whole heart and being into that song as if his existence was secondary and in service solely for that song flowing out of him. Every time he played that song, he felt alive. Even some of the drunks who were half-asleep at the tables raised their heads and turned towards him as if given life by the song itself.

'I think I've seen enough now,' he said, 'I think I know what you're trying to tell me.'

'I'm not supposed to tell you anything' I said, 'just making you see things for yourself.'

'You're saying that life isn't about living up to expectations. We can always find something interesting and worthwhile in whatever we do?'

I shrugged, 'I'm not here to convince you that life is worth living. There's no point since you're already dead. The point is to help you find peace. To get some perspective. And to go into the Transition with closure. So that you have no more regrets.'

'Then why did you show me the moment I made the worst decision of my life?'

'To tell you that it wasn't. Far from it. My job is to convince you to leave life without feeling like you've just lost. Because life isn't about winning, being rich or having a successful career. It's about being who you are. And at that moment, when you decided to go on tour with your band, you were being who you were, a musician. An artist. You dared to chase your dreams. But we can't deny that there are consequences if the goal is too elusive. At least you can make the best out of what you have since there is no going back.'

He was silent for a while, 'I guess that's what you were trying to tell me about Catherine too. I was in love with her, though it wasn't meant to be. But she did want to be friends with me. And our time at the conference shows that she accepted me for who I was.'

'Even if it isn't exactly the way you wanted. She accepted you regardless.'

My job was done. My subject had found his peace. I waited a few more minutes for all this to sink deeper into him, and then we waited together for the Transition.

'So, what can you tell me about what happens to me after the Transition?' he asked.

'As I already said, I don't know. But isn't it like life anyway? You make choices, but you don't know what's going to happen. So, whatever happens, you should just roll with it.'

'I suppose so.'

And then he was gone.

THE CRYING ANGEL

MH

This is one of those stories where someone finds a priceless treasure in the attic.

We found it among Gramp's dusty collection of paintings. He was convinced that one day they were going to be invaluable, even though it seemed obvious to us that a large portion of them wouldn't amount to much. But the painting of the crying angel... it was enchanting. It touched us, despite the lack of art appreciation in our veins.

Grace and I stood there in the store-room, sweaty and grimy and exhausted, but all we could think about was how outstanding the painting was. That someone was blessed with so much talent to be able to produce this piece of art. We stood there in silence for a long time, drawn towards the angel and her misery, allowing it to consume us.

I can still see it in my mind's eye now. The Angel covered her face as dark brown wavy hair ran down her shoulders. She was a picture of immeasurable grief, which infected us immediately. Her posture was that of grace, yet you could tell she was at her limits, just barely keeping herself whole amidst the melancholy. I could go on and on about how it moved us, about the hues and the lighting and the shades, but there aren't enough words to describe it.

It was Grace who broke the spell. 'It's beautiful, Mark. We... we have to tell your parents about it.'

I nodded numbly, not taking my eyes off the painting. Something this magical needs to be shared with the world, but there was a small part of me that was afraid it would be taken away from us.

At Grace's insistence, I showed Mum and Dad the painting. They too were awestruck, albeit to a smaller degree. Among the four of us, my love for the painting was the deepest. Dad suggested that we send it to be evaluated by experts. Right away, the part of me that loved the painting above everything else panicked. What if we lose it in the process? I knew it was illogical; the professionals would take better care of it than us, but I was still worried.

'You can send them a photo of it first,' Grace suggested, seemingly reading my mind. I suppose I have been incredibly lucky to have a girlfriend with a sound head on her shoulders, and we agreed it was a good idea.

That night, I moved the painting to my room and placed it against the wall opposite my bed. I kept studying the details of it. The angel's robe was incredibly life-like with its gentle folds, and her wings were drooping at just the right angle to convey a sense of hopelessness. I saw that her golden halo was beginning to dim from her sadness, and the clouds behind her drifted without strength, as if infected by her despair. I stared at it every night until I fell asleep, where I continued to see her weeping in my dreams.

It began rather mundanely. Aunt Melinda recommended us an art historian who was in the same university she was lecturing in. We emailed a photo of the painting to Dr.

Yates, who replied two days later telling us she needed to consult other professionals. Dad, who thought the painting might be our ticket to wealth, was disappointed. 'It couldn't be worth much after all. Otherwise, she would have replied with more enthusiasm,' he lamented.

Grace remained optimistic. 'It might not be the next "The Last Supper", but it must be worth something. She wouldn't have bothered if it wasn't.'

It turned out that they were both, in their own ways, wrong. The painting was more valuable than any of us could have predicted. In fact, some art critics thought it was more important that 'The Last Supper' or 'Mona Lisa', because it was one of only two oil paintings that Angelo Cavalcante, the artist who usually worked with watercolours, completed. His other oil painting was confirmed to have been destroyed during World War II, so 'The Crying Angel' was truly priceless.

The news spread like wildfire, and things went out of hand. Immediately, we were swarmed with requests from art historians, museums, collectors and auction houses to inspect the painting. Those who came were surprised by its good condition. Through some miracle, the painting had been largely untouched by damaging elements over the centuries. Initially, we froze at the inundation and the intrusion into our private lives, but finally one piece of the advice we received broke through our stupor. We agreed to hand the painting over to the professionals for safe-keeping — to prevent further degradation, and to avoid possible theft.

When they removed the painting from our house, a great sense of loss came over me, and I was morose the entire day. I could not sleep that night.

The painting had been in our family for generations, but after its presence was revealed to the world, we became targets. Plenty of offers, some of absurd amounts of money, floated in, but there were also criticisms. We were told that it was not our right to sell it; the painting belonged to the world. I never thought of it as an issue until strangers harassed us about our supposed selfishness for having the audacity to profit from the painting. There were plenty of comments urging us to donate it to an art museum, with the Louvre being one of the most frequently quoted.

Dad was peeved, of course. 'We are not going to donate it,' he declared firmly. Grace agreed that it would be crazy, but that did not stop the harassment. We were truly stressed out.

Then there were the private collectors. They started out calling and emailing us. Before long, they began turning up at our doorstep. Some of them sent representatives, but a few gave us the honour of shaking hands with some of the richest people on the planet by showing up personally, which made rejecting their offers harder.

My grades went down the drain. Grace was most alarmed since it was our plan for me to apply to the same university she was studying in to be with her. 'You need to focus, Mark. You are never going to be accepted at this rate,' she urged.

I told her I would make it work, but it was easier said than done. To be honest, it crossed my mind that since we were soon going to receive an obscene amount of money for the painting, why should I even bother with the university? It didn't help that suddenly I was the pillar of the family; Mum and Dad consulted me over every single message and mail we received. With so many options, we were in a constant state of confusion, ever more afraid of making the wrong decision.

As for the money. At first, the offers we got were in the range of a million dollars or so. As time went by and we were still saddled with indecision, some of the buyer candidates dropped out. This left only the serious contenders, and the price continued to climb. Five million, ten million, twelve million, fifteen million. We had never dealt with so much money before, and the pressure mounted. I knew that it would only be a matter of time before we faltered.

Eris appeared at our doorstep one day. Her dark hair was tied up into a tight bun, and she wore a sombre, black business suit. She was a little dark skinned, with sharp eyes that seemed to miss nothing and a voice that enchanted us. It was with this voice that she offered us an end to our conundrum. 'I'll take the painting off your hands, for thirty million dollars.'

Jaws dropped. Our highest offer up to that moment had been eighteen million. Only Grace kept her head. 'Wait, who are you exactly? Are you here for yourself or are you representing someone?'

I remembered feeling annoyed at Grace. At that moment, I was tempted to just take the offer, out of the belief that no one would be able to top it, and my desire to be done with this business. Yet, Grace was determined not to let us be fooled.

Eris looked rather annoyed, but she handed Grace her business card anyway. 'Let's just say I represent a group with a particular interest in the painting. We operate legally of course.'

My parents and I were lulled into a sense of trust, and we were too dumbstruck to protest. We behaved like innocent puppies, eager to please. Fortunately, Grace had the sense to ask Eris to leave the legal contract with us so that we could study it. Eris complied, but it was clear that she did not appreciate Grace's interference.

Strangely, all I remember now about that meeting was that Eris wore a golden apple around her neck and that she had a gap between her two front teeth. Everything else was murky. My parents too struggled to recall the details of the meeting, which heightened Grace's suspicion. We called up a few lawyers to check the documents, expecting them to find some loopholes that could destroy us. To our amazement, every one of them agreed that we were getting a legitimately advantageous deal.

'That sounds too good to be true,' Grace remarked when she heard the lawyers' opinions.

Once again, I grew irritated. 'So you know better?'

'It's not —'

'I don't understand why you keep finding problems when there are none,' I snapped. For the first time since we found the painting, I wished she would stay out of our business. That disagreement escalated into a big fight, and she returned to her campus for the new semester without seeing me again.

When Grace was out of the way, Eris visited us again. This time, my parents were totally won over. As for me, I suppose some of Grace's suspicion rubbed off on me, so I was not so quick to agree to Eris's offer.

'May I speak with Mark here in private?' Eris requested. My parents obediently left the room without a word.

'It's not that I don't trust you,' I said. 'It's just that, I don't know... what do you stand to gain from this? I doubt the painting is worth enough for you to turn a profit.'

Eris smiled seductively. 'I have my own reasons, but it's nothing you should be concerned about. I have less interest in profit than the other things I can do with the painting.'

'What other things?' I was curious, but also afraid.

Her eyes narrowed. 'You are beginning to sound like *her*. So full of suspicion.'

I kept quiet. That was the way we should be right, cautious? It bugged me that we did not have any of Grace's sense of apprehension when we were dealing with Eris; my parents would have sold their souls to her if she so much as suggested it to them.

Eris crossed her right leg over her left and leaned back in her chair. 'If you must know, here's my motivation: I know three people, gods among men, who would kill to get their hands on the painting. It is my intention to deny them the pleasure until I am ready to let one of them have it. As for you, they will get impatient soon, and they will come after you, and force you to choose one of them. But that's not all; in the process, you will be bribed, cajoled and threatened. In the end, choosing one means angering the other two. How do you like that prospect?'

In my mind, I saw my family being held hostage and forced to hand over the painting. It was terrifying; we wouldn't last an hour against such determined men. And what about Grace? She might be used against us too. With those grim images in my head, I promised Eris I would give her our answer the next day.

'Think carefully, Mark. The wrong decision could lead to war.' To my horror, she sounded satisfied, and her eyes were dark abysses that betrayed no compassion. As she walked away, there was a confidence to her stride that signalled the control she had over me. In contrast, I was feeling thoroughly defeated.

I spent the rest of the day thinking about Eris and her offer. I was increasingly convinced that I did not have a choice to begin with. After I had mulled over Eris's parting remarks, I called Grace to apologise and narrated everything that had transpired. When I was done, she sounded oddly calm. 'Mark, how good is your knowledge of Greek mythology?'

'Uh, I know Hercules, Hades and Zeus. Well, mainly the stuff from TV series and cartoons.'

Grace sighed. I bet she wondered how she ended up with an idiot like me. 'Eris and the golden apple, Mark.' She then gave me a summary of the tale about how Eris started a feud among the gods, which then led to the Trojan War.

'You mean, I am dealing with an actual Greek goddess?' I asked. By the time I realised how stupid it sounded, it was too late; I heard her sigh again.

'Good lord, of course not. My point is that this Eris Appleton could be heavily influenced by Greek mythology. Maybe she's one of those delusional rich people who treats this as a game. She's certainly not very subtle about her inspiration. One thing is for sure: you are in danger of being Paris of Troy if you have to choose who to sell the painting to.'

'What do you think I should do now?'

Grace sounded unsure when she replied, 'It's up to you, really. The painting belongs to your family. I'll still love you regardless of your decision.'

That cheered me up. It also made me realise how much stress the painting had inflicted on my family and me. 'What would you do if you were in my position?'

When she answered, it confirmed what I had already known.

I saw Eris for the last time when we signed the agreement. Mum and Dad were ecstatic. My future was secure. Eris shook my hand and smiled, showing the gap again. 'You couldn't have done any better. As far as choices go, you could have done a lot worse. By the way, it looks like you've got Athena by your side. Don't lose her.'

Grace and I continued to follow the news surrounding the painting. Of the three people Eris mentioned who were vying for the possession of the painting, none had a happy ending. As the painting passed from hand to hand, the first of them was murdered, the second filed for bankruptcy, and the third killed himself. This was followed by a few robberies, in which someone was shot and another kidnapped. Yet, the negativity surrounding the painting did not deter people from attempts to own it.

I watched the unfolding chaos with dread, but I knew that there was nothing I could have done to prevent it. It was not my destiny as a common mortal to interfere in the feuds of the gods. My role had simply been to discover the painting; everything had been set in motion the moment I spotted it in the storeroom. It seems absurd that a painting could cause so much destruction, but I still remember the feelings I had when I first laid eyes on it, and I think I can see its allure.

Occasionally, especially late at night, I replay the series of events in my head. I see Eris with the golden apple around her neck, smiling contentedly at the chaos she had unleashed. I think about the millions of dollars we now possess, and how they came at the expense of some ruined lives.

Most of all, I reflect on the painting and see as clear as day how the angel was burdened with all the grief in the world

I understand now why she weeps.

E.R.I.C

YK

My name is Eric. I got the incredibly rare chance to meet my Creator. Well, not in the meet-my-maker sense after death; I'm alive and well — so to speak. Not only did I meet my Creator, but I also got to know her, and even love her.

Of course, it all depends on what one means by 'love'. Because the thing is, your definition is most likely different from mine. It will be since you probably won't even think of me as real, and probably view my claim to love as untrue. In any case, I'll leave you to be the judge of that, once you have heard my story.

Insignificant. That's what I always was, and probably still am. I used to live in a small, single-room apartment, and I used to drive a small, beat-up car that could just barely fit four people. Every morning, from Monday to Friday, I would wake up at seven and drive to work.

My official job title was 'ODESolver', working in the Differential Equations Department. My manager would assign me a differential equation and my job was to solve it as fast as I could. The manager could be a real asshole sometimes. Every now and then, she wouldn't give me sufficient initial conditions, so that I couldn't even get started, and I would argue with her endlessly about it. Sometimes she would stop me while I was halfway through my job and tell me to discard all my results and to re-start with different initial data, wasting my effort.

You see, solving differential equations is no easy task since the equations can be complicated. I was only given the first set of numbers of the solution, and I had to use the differential equation to calculate the next set. Using the second set, I used the differential equations again to calculate the third set, then the fourth, fifth, sixth... By the time I was done, I would have a huge stack of papers containing thousands upon thousands of numbers which I then handed to the manager to stamp and sign before she passed it off to Printf, the department that took our results and sent them off to the clients.

That was pretty much my job. It was as mundane and boring as it sounds. I hated it. The bright part of my day came at 3 o'clock when the office would have a coffee break. I usually didn't join the others for lunch or coffee; during the coffee break, I would walk over to a café at the next block.

At that time of day, there were usually very few people at the café. The baristas were in no rush to take orders and were free to chat with the customers, which they normally did. And it was during that time that Eliza was usually there. I didn't know anything about her, other than the fact that she always talked to me with an easy smile and always remembered my order. Sometimes she would engage in idle conversation with me while I stood at the counter waiting for the other barista to make the coffee. She would talk about general, unimportant stuff like the weather or some current events. Sometimes she would gossip about other customers; that was fun. Then I would take my coffee to a table, sit down, and drink it alone. When my coffee break was over, I would walk back, dreading the thought of working a few more hours.

Work ended at 5 pm. Typically I would just head back home and cook dinner, then eat it while watching TV. Sometimes after dinner I would read a book, other times I would just keep watching TV until I fell asleep.

That was my life, one day after another. Over and over again. I hated it, and yet I never did anything to change it. I had no courage to quit my job or to find a new one, to get a better car or house, and I didn't even have the guts to ask Eliza for her phone number, much less for a date.

I can't explain why I didn't do all those things; I just became indifferent to it all. Or maybe it was because I was getting old and tired. I can't tell you how old I am because that concept, when communicated from me to you, has no meaning. Again, it depends on your definition of 'old' since if you don't think I'm real, how could I be *old*? Anyway, with me, time does not have the same meaning as you think. In any case, I did feel old, at least, in the sense that I was already beyond my prime. I got tired easily and became sick more often. I could feel my body decaying. Changing jobs, buying a new house, going on dates, or even socialising in general, felt like new adventures not worth the effort. So I remained indifferent, not bothering to start a new life or even 'living a life'. Somehow, I decided to wait for this one to end. That would be it.

Chekhov once said that indifference is the paralysis of the soul; a premature death.

But I never had a soul to begin with! At least, that's probably what you would say, dear reader. I'll leave you to be the judge of that too. Premature death? Ha! I was never alive to begin with!

Anyway, that was how I passed my days before I started having the dreams.

The dreams were strange. They always felt so real and lucid that I didn't know they were dreams until I woke up in my bed. They were all the same: I would inexplicably

57

find myself handcuffed to a metal chair, sitting in the centre of a square room with cement walls. There was a door in the wall facing me. The room was illuminated by a harsh light coming from a bulb hanging just a few inches above me. I looked around and struggled against my handcuffs, which were attached to my left hand. I tried pulling on them with my right hand, but of course that didn't do anything. I wanted to call out but realised that I couldn't speak.

Then the door would open, and I could see a figure entering the room, but I couldn't see the face clearly because of the light dazzling my eyes. In fact, I couldn't even tell if the person was a man or a woman.

The figure paced in front of me.

'Hello, Eric.' Even from the voice I couldn't tell whether it was a man or a woman.

'Who are you?' was all I could muster. Strangely, despite being cuffed to a chair with an unknown figure pacing in front of me, I was not scared all. In fact, when the character appeared I felt strangely calm and relaxed. Even serene. I thought I might have been drugged.

'I'm Scott,' the figure said.

'Scott,' I repeated, 'I'm Eric.'

'Can you tell me anything about yourself?'

'There's nothing really interesting about me,' I said meekly, 'I work at the Numerical Research Centre.'

'What do you do?'

'I'm an ODESolver,' I said, then felt compelled to explain some details about my work.

'How's your commute to work?'

'How?' I remembered being puzzled by his questions. I assumed this interrogator was a man since he said his name was Scott. Somehow, I felt the need to answer him honestly.

'Are you asking if I drive to work? Well yeah, I drive.'

He seemed to ignore my response. Then he asked, 'how many legs does a cow have?'

'Four? What's this got to do with any —'

'How many legs does a centipede have?'

'It's called a centipede,' I said, 'so you might expect me to say it has a hundred legs. But it doesn't.'

'How many does it have, then?'

'It can't have a hundred legs exactly. A healthy centipede has an odd number of pairs of legs.'

'How did you know that?'

'I saw it on QI.'

'What's QI?'

'It's a TV show; it stands for Quite Interesting. Why are you asking me all these questions?'

Then I would wake up, realising that it was just a dream. I would check the clock and see that it was close to the time I was supposed to wake anyway, so I would get out of bed and start the day.

The dreams started happening more frequently. The only thing that changed were the names of my interrogators. Sometimes it was Scott, other times it was Priya or Susan. Half the time the interrogators didn't even bother to introduce themselves. I could never make out their faces or any of their physical characteristics.

The questions started to change too, more difficult to answer. Instead of simple, factual questions such as the number of legs on a centipede, the interrogators started asking about vague stuff like the purpose of life and emotions.

'Tell me about jealousy,' one interrogator asked.

'Tell you how? Do you want me to define it?'

'Have you ever been jealous of someone before?'

'I have, sure. Many times,' I said. Though I was compelled to be honest, I didn't feel like revealing personal stories about myself at first, 'sometimes you see people having things you could never have, and feel a little hurt by it.'

'Why do we feel hurt by these things?'

'Because jealousy is a reminder that life is unfair, and that you got the shit end of the deal. It's the moment when you realise the universe is treating you like crap, and you're angry about it.'

'Universe? Do you mean God?'

'No. I'm not getting into that debate. But you know what I mean.'

Despite the dreams, my waking life continued as usual. At first. But all those questions about jealousy and other emotions seemed to make me a little more contemplative.

One day my manager got transferred to another department, and Charlie, who worked at my office as a PDESolver, was promoted in her place. Charlie recently got married. I only knew this because he sent me an invitation which I ignored. I wasn't close to him at all. In fact, I didn't even like him.

I had worked in this department longer than him, and, forgive me, dear reader, for being so bold as to say — I was better at the job than him. You could verify this for yourself. My output rate was much faster than his ever was. In his first few years here he was terrible at his job, constantly coming to my desk with questions. Many times, I had to put my own jobs on hold to help him.

I guess it was my fault, really. I didn't socialise much with the bosses.

I mostly kept to myself when I first met him. I found his charm false and insincere. And now, dear reader, I am ashamed to admit that I resented him when he got promoted over my head, got married, and bought a beautiful house.

My frustrations started bleeding into my dreams. One night the interrogator asked what I hated the most.

'Insincerity,' I said.

'Why do you say —'

'People being rewarded for their insincerity. *That's* what I hate the most.'

As I recall, it was the first time I interrupted the interrogator in a dream. However, I still failed to recognise it as a dream until I woke up.

'It's how society works,' I said, 'but I hate it.'

'What do you mean by insincerity being rewarded?'

'You know how some people suck up to bosses to get a promotion or a business deal? Or how people make contacts at parties. And these people help each other to get business and jobs.'

'It's called "networking",' said the interrogator.

'Yes. And I hate it.'

'Why?'

'Because what eventually happens is that you get these fucking lowlifes going around being friendly and chatty with people just to get ahead in life. People become successful not because they're good at their jobs; they succeed just because they have many connections.'

'Being friendly for the sake of self-interest,' the interrogator seemed to agree.

'Yes,' I said, then I started telling the interrogator about Charlie. The interrogator just stood there listening quietly. Faceless and motionless.

'I didn't want to play tennis with the bosses because I don't have much in common with them, or share the same interests. If I socialised with them, it would have been insincere. I would have been doing it for selfish reasons.'

Then, something new happened that had not occurred before in the previous dreams. The interrogator was silent for an unusually long time. Then the interrogator left the room, leaving me alone. Even at that moment, still not knowing yet that I was dreaming, I found that odd. I sat there waiting. I pulled my hand against the handcuffs and started looking around. I still couldn't see much because of the light on my face. Only my left hand was cuffed, so I reached out with my right to try and turn the light away.

Here's the funny thing. Initially, I thought the lamp was just a few inches from my face. But as I reached out as far as I could, I couldn't touch anything! I had assumed that it was some lamp or light fixture hanging from the ceiling, but I couldn't see any wires or poles to the bulb. Soon I questioned whether it was an electric bulb at all. All I could see was some light. Harsh and bright.

I found myself unable to concentrate on work the next day. Everything seemed to grate on my nerves. Charlie, looking comfortable and smug in his new manager's office. My desk, strewn with lists of numbers. The vapid chatter of the other Solvers from across the room. Overwhelming and unbearable.

When it was time for the coffee break, I went to the café, hoping to see Eliza as usual. But this time she was not there. Some other barista took my order, and I sat down at a table. There was a large group of men sitting at the next table, being loud and rowdy, adding to my tension. I just glared at them while I drank my coffee. That only lasted a while before some impulse made me yell, 'Keep it down!'

'Fuck you,' one of them replied, and continued to eat his pastry as they kept talking.

As I headed back to the office, I noticed the rowdy group following me. Soon they caught up and surrounded me.

'What's your problem, dude?' one of them said.

'I don't know, you're the one who's following me.'

Suddenly I saw stars, as a sharp pain pierced the back of my head. Then the guy who was talking to me punched me in the stomach. I fell onto the sidewalk.

Now, usually I'm not a brave person. I'm very much of a coward. But on that day, that particular afternoon, positively hating my life and my job, I just didn't care anymore.

I saw a loose brick on the ground. I picked it up and tried to swing it at his head. I missed.

After that, they wouldn't stop pummelling me.

I woke up in that room again. The one I had in my dreams, but this time I still felt the pain from the beatdown those assholes gave me. The light on my face obscured the approaching figure, as usual.

'What were you thinking?' said the figure.

'I don't know. I wasn't, I guess.'

'It seems like you hate your life these days.'

'I've always hated my life.'

The figure was silent for a moment. Then it said, 'I'm sorry.'

'Don't feel sorry for me. Who are you anyway?'

'I'm not feeling sorry for you; I'm apologising.'

'Why? Are you one of the guys who beat me up?'

Another pause. This time it was much longer. Then the figure said, 'No, but it's my fault, because I created you... Eric... are you okay?'

'Yeah.'

'Did you understand what I said?'

'That you created me? No. I just want to wake up now.'

'This is not a dream, Eric. This is happening right now.'

'Are you saying you are God?'

'No.' The figure started pacing in front of me. The bright lights were still on my face, and I couldn't see clearly.

'I'm not God,' the figure said, 'but I created you, and this world. The city, streets, everything.'

'I don't understand.'

'The Room... not this room, but the world you're living in. It's called the Room because that's how it started out.'

I was silent and confused. The figure seemed to give a little laugh, saying, 'I don't know how to explain. Anyway, the Room is a computer program, an operating system written for AI bots to interact with each other and evolve.'

'Are you saying that I am a...'

'You're my first, Eric. My proudest work. You're the first artificial intelligence program that has passed the Turing Test.'

'So, I'm not real?'

'That's not true. You are real. To everyone in this world, and to me!'

'Huh.'

'You seem to be taking all this really well, considering.'

'I have a question, though. Why can't I see your face?'

'It's because I haven't got an avatar loaded. Would you like me to load one?'

'Yes, please.'

'Hold on a sec, I'm gonna have to dig around this computer,' said the figure as it stopped pacing and stood motionless, still bathed in the bright light.

A few moments later, the light dimmed, and the rest of the room became visible. As the glare faded away, the figure's face gradually came into focus. It was...

'You're Scarlett Hansson?'

'No, I'm not. I just happened to find that avatar on Scott's computer. He must be a fan. I wonder what he uses it for...,' there was a brief pause, then, 'Ew! No no no. I'm not using this avatar.'

The bright lights came back and 'Scarlett' dissolved into a featureless, faceless figure again. 'Let me pause you while I scan myself into an avatar.'

'Pause me?' I asked as instantly the lights dimmed to normal levels and I could see a young woman standing in front of me.

A square table with two chairs appeared between us, and the grey walls of the room turned brown, and I could see the room getting bigger. One side of the wall disappeared completely, being replaced by a large window. I could see traffic on the street outside the window, and I realised that I recognised that street and the room. It was the café!

'I thought you'd be more comfortable if I put us in your favourite café,' she said.

Being in that café made me instinctively turn around to look at the counter.

'She doesn't work here anymore,' she said, 'Got a clerical job at Teslaware.'

'You're omnipotent and omniscient. So, you're really are God.'

She gave a little laugh, 'No! I just ran an *object_place( )* command to put us here. For Eliza, I simply ran a search. I didn't know where she was until I did the search.'

'But you knew I was looking for her when I looked at the counter.'

'Because I was watching you. Whoops, that probably sounded creepy, but I wrote the code you run on. I was keeping track of your progress, so I know most of your daily routine.'

'If you wrote me and I'm your computer program, then... then can you read my mind? I'm a code to you, right? You can just read it.'

'No,' she shook her head, 'I can't. As an AI, your code — your mind, is as complex as any human brain.' As she talked, she moved her hands around like she was holding an invisible ball and wriggled her fingers, 'I can't read your mind any more than I can understand the electrical signals firing all over someone else's brain.'

'But you said you watched me. Do you mean you can see anywhere in this world? Are you always everywhere?'

'No. I can only check in on a place at a time. You're my first working AI, so I wrote a script to keep track of you in particular.'

'Why did you reveal yourself to me? Why now?'

'Because you got into pretty serious trouble with those three guys. I had to step in. Before today, you never got into any problems like this.'

'I've been in a kind of weird place in my life lately.'

'Remember, though. I'm not God. I'm not omnipotent, so I may not be able to bail you out every single time. You need to take care of yourself.'

'Yeah, sure. I have one more question, though.'

'Go ahead. Shoot.'

'What's your name?'

'Cassidy Winters.'

'Nice to meet you, Cassidy. Guess you already know my name.'

'Yes, I know your name. In fact, there's something about your name you probably don't know about yet.'

'What is it?'

'Your name. It's an acronym. It stands for Evolutionary Retro-cognitive Intelligence Code. E.R.I.C.'

Cassidy was right. I seemed to have taken all this in really well. Neo in the Matrix vomited when he was told his whole life was a simulation. I didn't; I just proceeded to have coffee with the person who claimed to have created me. I know what some of you might say: probably that's just because I'm an emotionless machine. Of course I couldn't react the same way as Neo did. He was human.

I may not be human, but you can't deny that just before Cassidy revealed herself to me, I had very human emotions — I hated my life.

Things did get a little better after she revealed herself to me. I didn't hate my job as much as I used to, knowing that all the bullshit with Charlie and everyone else at my job wasn't actually 'real'. The job itself was still important, though. My work in the Differential Equations Department did serve a purpose for Cassidy and her colleagues. The equations that we solved were used in their applications in physics and engineering. Sometimes even for chemistry and biology. So, in this strange way, knowing that my world wasn't 'real', but my job was, gave me a sense of purpose and determination. I worked harder than ever, knowing that it was important to Cassidy.

I stopped talking to Charlie and everyone else at work. I just ignored them.

Cassidy seemed happy with my work. I guess that's all that mattered, as she was the Creator. Since that day, we began meeting regularly on the bridge that I used to walk between my work and the café. It turned out that we both liked standing close to large bodies of water. Lakes and rivers were particularly appealing to both of us. It's a funny thing, for sure. But for me, I seemed to like it because it seemed peaceful and orderly, quite unlike the harsh jaggedness of buildings and hard ground. Clearly, I had many questions about the world she had created, my world. She told me it started as an undergraduate project she worked on five years ago. That's five years of Cassidy's time, since I experience time differently in here.

Speaking of time, one day we spent almost an entire afternoon talking about how to define time for my world. My world is simulated on a supercomputer that runs at about 150 petaflops, or 150 quadrillion Floating Point Operations per second. An iteration cycle takes up about 350 megaflops, and a 'day' is about ten billion iteration cycles.

So, doing the calculation, which includes various down-times and resets and reboots, we've estimated that I have been working on this job for an equivalent of eight years. Which kind of explains why I'm so sick of it.

'It's not bad, being tired of a job after eight years,' she said, 'I've been at this for five years, and it's starting to get on my nerves.'

'That means *I'm* getting on your nerves. Because quite literally I am your work.'

'Of course it's not you. It's the things outside this world that get on my nerves. The people. I hate people,' she gave a small chuckle as she said that.

'Tell me about the world outside.'

'It sucks. Economy's going to hell. Almost every week there's news about a terrorist attack, or someone going nuts and stabbing people. And, I've already said this, but people are horrible.'

One day, we were at the bridge again with Cassidy looking happy.

'Guess what,' she said, 'you're a star!'

I asked her what she meant by that, and she said, 'So, remember the dreams you had where you were on a chair, with people asking you questions?'

'Yeah, that grey room. I haven't had those dreams in a while. Did you have something to do with that?'

Suddenly her smile faded a little bit, telling me that she did have something to do with it. Then she hesitated for a while. 'It's okay,' I said, 'can you tell me why I had those dreams?'

'It was a Turing test,' she said, 'it's a test where people ask questions to an Artificial Intelligence, to see whether the AI can fool the tester by answering the questions like a human being.'

'So, that's what it was? Putting me on a chair in a middle of the night and asking me weird questions? Is that why it was a different voice each time? Because different people were coming in to talk to me?'

'Yes.'

We were silent for about a minute, before she finally said, 'You're angry.'

'Those dreams messed me up. I couldn't focus on my job for days.'

'I'm sorry, I thought placing you in an alternative environment would separate the effects of... I'm sorry, Okay?'

'Okay, I guess. I mean, you're my Creator. You can do whatever you want. Being mad at you would be like blasphemy or something.'

'Cut it out with that God bullshit.'

'As you command, I will.'

'Eric, come on.' It was clear she was getting annoyed by this.

'Okay, sorry. I'm kidding. Let's back up. Why am I a star?'

'The Turing test. You passed it. All those people that came to talk to you. You've convinced them!'

'Convince them of what?'

'That you're... you know...?'

'That I'm real?'

'That you are intelligent.'

'Thanks, but I don't know why that feels insulting.'

'I know, it's weird for the both of us. We both know that you're you. But everyone else... they don't know you really exist. You have feelings and your own opinions and stuff. You just got mad at me.'

'I still am. A bit.'

I did not see Cassidy for a few days after that. But during that time, I felt very conflicted about the idea of being 'mad' at Cassidy. I wondered if I had a right to be angry at her. At first, I felt like a spoiled kid being mad at their parents, but ultimately it is the parents who are right and know best. Perhaps a better analogy for my case would be a human being angry at God, losing their faith or something. But Cassidy didn't 'work in mysterious ways' the way that religious deities are supposed to. She flat-out told me everything about this world. I was her research project. A pretty successful one, it seemed. I was the first Artificial Intelligence to pass the Turing test. She created me with that express purpose to do that. So, what right did I have to be angry at her?

A few days later, as I was leaving work to drive home, I saw Cassidy waiting for me by my car. She held up a DVD.

'Let's not chat this time,' she said, 'I don't want you getting mad at me again. Let's watch a movie together.'

'I'm just a computer program that you wrote. Why do you care how I feel?'

'Of course I care,' she said, 'I created you. Same way mums don't want their kids to stay mad at them.'

'Is that what this is? You're my mum?'

'Ugh, I regret that analogy. I don't want kids.'

'Well, be glad you didn't have to change my diaper.' That made her chuckle a bit.

'Shut up and drive us home, will ya?'

We drove back to my house, and we watched *Far From the Madding Crowd*. It was a movie based on a Thomas Hardy book. She said it was one of her favourites. It was about an independent, free-spirited woman who denied proposals from three different men.

'Bathsheba Everdene,' I said, 'she has the coolest name.'

'She is cool.' said Cassidy, 'She's independent and can run a big farm as well as any man. I like that. I wish I could be more like her.'

'But you are. You literally run my entire world.'

'This world pretty much runs itself. I don't have to do much these days. I just check the parameters from time to time.'

'So, do you have three guys proposing to you too? Like Bathsheba had?' I asked, then regretted it. It was the first time I ever asked her a personal question.

'No, none. Though I wish everyone in my world would believe that a woman like me could create the first AI to pass the Turing test.'

'Seriously? People still have a problem with that?'

'Well, to be fair I don't really know if it's because I'm a woman or not. But my professor seems to be taking most of the credit in the press.'

'Press, huh. You weren't kidding about me being a star.'

'The news picked it up soon after we published the paper about you. The headlines all say "Austrian professor in Singapore invents first Artificial Intelligence".'

'That sucks.'

'Yeah, but that's fine, I guess. We shouldn't care what other people think about ourselves. I know my value, and that's enough.'

Cassidy wasn't kidding about the press. I agreed to be interviewed by the journalists, though I asked Cassidy to put me in the café instead of the grey interrogation room.

'Hi, I'm Deena Takur, from AG News,' said the journalist, shaking my hand. Of course, I was just shaking her avatar's hand.

'I know your work. AG News is one of my favourite channels on YouTube.'

'Oh, really? Glad to hear that!' said Takur, 'Dr. Schwarz says that you use the internet just like the rest of us.'

'Yes, I do. I read books and watch movies too. Everyone seems to be surprised by that.'

'Do you have a favourite book?'

I thought for a moment, then named *The Picture of Dorian Gray,* but added, 'A more apt book would be Shelley's *Frankenstein*, even though I didn't like it much. Too depressing.'

'That's funny because Ms. Winters said she learned an important lesson from that book. She vowed never to repeat Victor Frankenstein's mistake of abandoning her creation.'

'Oh, did she? That's nice.' *Cassidy would never abandon me,* I thought.

'There is something that we humans always wonder about, but will probably never know the answer to. How did you feel about meeting your own Creator? Was there panic? Excitement? Existential crisis?'

'To be honest, I'm not the right person to ask. Sorry, I used the word "person", I'm just used to —'

'No, I think "person" is the right word to use,' she said.

'Thanks. I don't know how to answer your question. Because the day I found out who I really was, I was in... I was in a depressed state. In a way, I was already in some sort of existential crisis before I knew the truth. My life sucked, and I didn't see the point in anything I did. When Cassidy showed up, it strangely made me feel a little bit more normal. I started going to work on time, started seeing friends. I guess knowing my Creator made me feel less burdened, somehow.'

Despite learning her lesson from *Frankenstein*, she did leave me after all. Though it was in a way which I hardly noticed. I got 'paused' after she was gone. So, I didn't feel her absence, but she did feel mine. The last time I spoke to Cassidy was when she came in to tell me she was getting her PhD. Most of her thesis was about me and the simulated world I lived in. She thanked me for telling all the journalists who interviewed me that she wrote all my codes by herself, and the fact that Schwarz was against the project at first.

It was a goodbye of sorts. She said she was leaving computer science to find a job in a different industry. I thought it was a waste, seeing that she had just got her PhD and all, but she told me she had had enough of the field. She was sad to leave me, though. I asked her to take me with her, wherever she was planning to go. But it was impossible. I was hard-coded into the university servers. She would have to leave me behind with Professor Schwarz.

Despite the press attention Cassidy and I got for the department, Schwarz was not interested in keeping me and my world running. Funding was cut for the project that created me, and I was subsequently 'turned off'.

As you might know, the only reason I was switched back on was to talk to Cassidy one last time, when she was 89 years old and on her deathbed.

'Did you get your three suitors like Bathsheba?' I asked her.

'I had some, but I turned them all down.'

'So, you never had any kids?'

'No, Eric. You're basically my only son.'

'You say you hate being called my mum, but you keep bringing that up.'

ONLY ONE IN THE WORLD

MH

Linda tapped her feet impatiently. She was getting hungry, and it didn't seem like the customer in front of her would be done soon.

'I would like to have set A as well, with coleslaw as the side. Can I have the chicken breast?' she heard the man say.

The cashier keyed in the order as the man looked at the menu again. Linda rolled her eyes; why can't people make up their minds before going up to the counter? Once again, her right foot moved restlessly.

'Wait, I'll like to change that to set C instead,' the man called out, during which Linda suppressed a groan. Her only consolation was that the cashier, possibly a part-timer based on his looks, shared her feelings of annoyance as he gestured for the manager to cancel the order.

Two minutes later, the man was still debating on whether he wanted apple soda or grape soda. By then, Linda was getting angry. She did not come to a fast food restaurant to wait forever to get her food. Part of her was annoyed that Kim's Fried Chicken had only one counter open, but mostly she was irritated with the man's indecisiveness. She could tell that the customers behind her were also getting impatient, but it was not as if they could do anything about it.

77

'But I can, can't I?' Linda thought. Then there was the question of whether she should. Does the man deserve what she was about to do to him, just because he held up the line?

At that moment, the man's order was completed. He handed over some notes, gathered his purchases and turned around to leave. It was finally Linda's turn, and she sighed in relief. She stepped up to the counter and nodded at the equally exasperated cashier. 'Having here, miss?'

'Take-away,' Linda replied. 'I'd like to have two set D's. Drinks, apple soda for both.' The teenager smiled and keyed in her order, and just as he was about to reach for the tray behind him, the earlier customer returned.

'Eh, mister, I ordered six apple sodas and one orange soda. You gave me two orange,' the man complained, as he jostled past Linda and occupied her space.

It was the last straw. Linda felt a burning anger that morphed into an uncontrollable hatred. The man remained oblivious, but Linda silently put every iota of her disdain into her stare. She reached into the dark space in her mind and wished.

And wished, and wished, and wished.

When it was done, she mustered a small smile. The man, satisfied at last, strode out of the place. The cashier apologised to Linda, and hurriedly assembled her orders. Out of the corner of her eye, she saw the man make his way to the bus-stop right in front of the shop. He was still standing there checking his orders when moments later, Linda walked out and made her way to the overhead pedestrian crossing further down the street.

She was halfway across when she looked down and saw the man trip. He fell onto the road, with his bags of takeaway food, into the path of an incoming bus.

Linda heard the screams from other bystanders, but she did not bother to look. Only one person had survived her wishes before, and she knew it in her heart that this man would not be the second.

'Took you long enough,' Michelle grumbled. Linda ignored her sister and proceeded to place the food onto two plates. She would have told Michelle about the man, but since Michelle had the same gift for wishing death unto others, it seemed pointless.

'There should only be one,' Linda thought scornfully. 'Me, me, me.'

'I made soup,' Michelle announced, as she wheeled herself towards the stove. She had been paralysed from the waist down ever since their father, in a fit of drunken wrath, had thrown the then twelve-year-old down the stairs. In retaliation, Michelle had made her wish, and their father died of an embolism that very night.

Their mother's mistake was in being too perceptive. When people around the girls started dying in freak accidents, and of unnatural causes, she became suspicious. She had no evidence, of course; the special thing about the gift was that the girls did not even need to be around the victims to cause their deaths. Yet, the girls knew that having their mother around was only going to be a hindrance.

One night, in their bedroom, the girls spoke in hushed whispers. At long last, they played rock-paper-scissors. Linda had put out scissors. Michelle's clenched fist meant that Linda was the one who had to make the wish. It was difficult, because their mother, other than being guilty of turning a blind eye towards the abuse their father heaped on them, was not a bad person. Still, Linda put all her determination into her wish. Two nights later, their mother was electrocuted while taking a shower.

Now, as the two sisters sat in the living room, eating their dinners in front of the television, their minds began to fill with hatred for each other. 'There should only be one of us,' each of them thought. However, no matter how hard they wished for each other's death, nothing seemed to work. It turned out that having the ability to wish death onto others granted them immunity towards it.

Inevitably, the local news turned to the topic of the man who got hit by a bus. Michelle gestured at the television and asked, 'Was that your wish?'

'Yes,' Linda replied, taking another spoonful of soup.

'That's a waste of your gift.'

'He annoyed me.'

Michelle remained silent, but her eyes bore into her older sister's skull. She continued to make her wish, as she had been doing for years. When she saw Linda's eyebrows knit themselves into a frown, she began to wish harder. 'Me, me, me. There should only be me.'

Linda's right hand went up to her throat. She coughed, and felt her throat tighten. She turned around in anger and desperation, even as she tried to breathe. Michelle managed to dodge as Linda hurled the bowl of soup at her.

'We've wished for each other's death for so long, it's time I take matters into my own hand,' Michelle said. Her eyes were emotionless. She pulled out a knife from the side of her wheelchair.

Despite her weakened state, Linda scrambled away from her murderous sister. Michelle furiously turned the wheel of her wheelchair to go after her, but Linda, now wheezing for breath, managed to make it into the kitchen. In desperation, she filled a glass with water from the tap and tried to drink. It was hard to swallow, but she managed to sip some.

Michelle tried to reach Linda, but being able-bodied, the older woman had an advantage. She climbed onto the counter top and kicked out at Michelle. The knife sank into her shin, but her kick connected with Michelle's knee and sent her reeling backwards. Linda cried out in pain as a thin stream of blood flowed freely from her wound.

'Me, me, me.' Those words rang out in both their minds, but they sounded particularly encouraging for Michelle. Undaunted, she tried again. After all, she still had the knife in her hand, and Linda was still trying to breathe. This time though, Linda was a lot more composed; her hand thrashed wildly around her, hoping to find a weapon. The knives were out of reach, but her fingers closed around a solid metal handle. Just as Michelle's blade slashed frantically at her, she swung the saucepan hard. There was a clang as the saucepan collided with the knife.

With both sisters refusing to give up, each wishing harder and harder, the only way for either of them to survive was to pit their physical strengths against one another. Michelle, with years of training hauling herself in and out of her wheelchair, had stronger arms, but Linda had functional legs.

Another desperate stab from Michelle. This time, Linda swung the saucepan at Michelle's wrist. There was a dull thud, and she saw the knife fall out of Michelle's hand and skid across the tiled floor. It was her chance. 'Me, me, me,' she thought as she leapt off the counter.

Michelle clawed at her, and her nails dug into Linda's shoulder. With her throat still constricted, Linda had little strength left. Once again, the saucepan played its part in the skirmish. This time, the utensil landed on Michelle's head. The clawing stopped for a moment, allowing Linda to attempt a deep breath. She thought she was going to die; it did not seem like her airways would open again.

'But I am special,' she reaffirmed and refused to be defeated. 'There can only be one, and that will be me.'

Dazedly, Michelle tried to reach for another knife, but Linda, with all her ferocity, hit her across the face with the saucepan. This time, she had swung so hard that the pan flew out of her hand. For a moment, in her weaponless state, she thought it was the end. It took her a while to register that Michelle was already unconscious.

'ME! ME! THERE CAN ONLY BE ME!' The voice in Linda's head was deafening now. Her lungs were still begging for air, but she could feel a crazy laughter rising in her. She opened the kitchen drawer and pulled out the cast-iron frying pan.

'There can only be one of us,' she rasped. She lifted the pan above her head and then brought it down on Michelle's head as hard as she could. Again, and again, and again.

When it was all over, Linda's face and the front of her dress were soaked with blood. Michelle's head was nothing but a bloody mess. Suddenly, her throat cleared, and she could breathe normally again.

'THE SPECIAL ONE IS... ME!' Linda cried out with a mad giggle. 'I have always known it, since...since...' She searched her memory. Since when? Was it when their father kicked her when she was five? Was it when he slammed Michelle against her crib when she was a mere toddler? Was it when their mother turned a deaf ear to their pleas for help? Or was it the time her father twisted her ear so hard it almost came off?

It didn't matter anymore, Linda decided. After all, there was only her now. She brought her bloodied hands to her face, and as they slid down to her neck, she laughed again.

Me, me, me.

MEMORY INC.

MH

Marissa cringed as the tiny crabs rushed back into their respective holes. Their scurrying movements made her skin crawl, and she held on tightly to Vanessa's hand.

'Don't be afraid. They won't disturb you,' Vanessa assured her. Vanessa took two steps forward, dragging Marissa along, and then stomped on the sandy ground. A few more crabs ran across the sand and disappeared into the many holes they had dug. 'It's kind of cute, don't you think?'

Marissa giggled nervously. The beach looked huge to her five-year-old self, and the waves looked like sets of teeth rushing to meet her. 'Come along,' Vanessa urged, tugging at her hand, as she made her way towards the waterline.

'I'm scared. Don't let go of me,' Marissa said. She felt as if the waves were going to consume her, roaring and chomping, but Vanessa managed to persuade her little sister anyway. Before long, Marissa was laughing and shrieking with joy every time a wave pounded her. Vanessa too was laughing, and she kept her promise; not once did she let go of Marissa's hand.

Once they had enough of splashing in the sea, the girls went on to build sandcastles. It was a disaster; they could not seem to get the right sand consistency to create anything other than a dispirited lump. Too wet and the sand was as good as mud; too dry and it was crumbling no matter how they packed it. Yet, they had a lot of fun, and even their parents, usually uptight and severe, were enjoying themselves.

Their time at the beach resort seemed to last forever. At least that was how Marissa remembered it to be. When it was time for them to leave, Marissa started crying. 'We have to go home,' her father explained in exasperation. That did not stop the tears. In the end, it was Vanessa who managed to cheer Marissa up with a promise of candies.

'Silly girl, we'll have to go home eventually,' Vanessa explained in the car. She had one hand around Marissa's shoulders.

'I don't want to leave. I want to spend happy times with you,' Marissa said.

I want to spend happy times with you.

The spell broke, and Marissa woke up. She looked at the clock and realised that it was almost time for her to get up for work. Her heart was filled with longing; she wished she could stay in that dream… no, it was a memory, wasn't it?… forever. At least Vanessa was there, and they were happy.

Still, the trip down memory lane brought a smile to her face. It had been months since she had the strength to smile, but those pills did the trick. With a sudden burst of enthusiasm, she got up and showered. To her parents' surprise, she was on time for the first time since Vanessa's death.

Marissa hummed to herself as she rearranged the CD cases on her shelf. In the digital age where songs can be obtained through a single click, those CDs had lost their purpose, but she hung on to them anyway, as with every-thing else related to Vanessa. In the two weeks since she started taking the pills, she had gotten more energetic. After all, she had something to look forward to every day now.

Her mother peered into the room. While she was ini-tially elated at the change in Marissa's temperament, she was getting concerned. 'Marissa? Are you alright?'

'Yes, Mum,' Marissa replied. She forced a smile. She could tell that her mother was getting suspicious, but she hoped that she wouldn't broach the subject.

'You seem... different.'

Another smile. 'I realised that even though Vanessa is gone, I still have the memories I shared with her, and when I really miss her I can just uhm... revisit those mem-ories. It's enough to get me out of this slump.'

Her mother broke into a smile of relief. She went over to her younger daughter and gave her a tight hug. Marissa returned the hug half-heartedly, her eyes already fixed on the drawer in which she hid the pills.

Vanessa pretended to pour tea from the plastic teapot into Marissa's tiny cup. 'Here's your tea, Miss,' she said. She then placed the empty plastic plate in front of Maris-sa. 'And your spaghetti.'

'Thank you. The bill please,' Marissa replied in an af-fected posh tone.

'Ten dollars,' Vanessa declared.

Marissa dug into the purse and frowned at the wad of fake paper money in her hands. 'There are no ten dollar bills here.'

'Order another set then,' Vanessa suggested, grinning broadly and displaying her terribly crooked teeth.

She fixed those teeth with braces when she was fifteen. I was told to do the same, but I was too much of a coward to do it, even though Vanessa assured me it wouldn't hurt much.

Suddenly, Marissa was aware that this make-believe tea party was merely a fragment of her memory from the time she was seven, and it made her uncomfortable. She shook her head and tried to push the intruding thought away. She struggled to return to the first-person point of view her seven-year-old self-inhabited, but it was too late. Her surroundings changed, and they were playing cards instead.

Vanessa threw out a pair of threes. 'Your turn.'

I asked Vanessa if playing with cards was gambling. I was worried about the police arresting us. She explained that it was not gambling if no money was involved.

There it was again, another errant thought ruining her experience. Squeezing her eyes shut, Marissa desperately resisted the encroachment of the present. She stared at the cards in her hands. They were all blank. She blinked, and they came into focus. Vanessa looked impatient, and Marissa settled on putting out a pair of Queens.

'You know, I don't really want to grow up. I don't think I'll like to work. Dad told me work is a hassle and that school is more fun,' Vanessa said as she put out a pair of aces.

'Pass,' Marissa said. 'But there's homework to do, and sometimes the teacher scolds you.'

'Not if you are good; teachers only punish you when you are naughty.'

Yeah, Vanessa was the teacher's pet. She was always obedient, quiet and her grades were good. She wasn't perfect, of course, but she knew how to pretend *to be perfect. She threw her tantrums in front of me, but never in front of the adults. She hid her rage in their presence and then released it on inanimate objects in her room. In that sense, she was perfect for this pretentious world.*

Before Marissa could do anything, her world turned black. When she opened her eyes, it was morning, time for her to get ready for work. Marissa reached for the framed photo of her dead sister on her bedside table, clasped it to her chest, and cried.

Heart pounding, Marissa dialled the number she had saved under 'Memory Inc.' While waiting for her call to be picked up, the motto of the company rang in her head: 'Relive your memories!' In hindsight, the whole setup seemed shady as hell. Unfortunately, she was already hooked.

'Hello, Memory Inc. How may we help you?'

'Hi.... I'm uh, Marissa. I need to speak to Dr. Max,' Marissa said. She tapped her feet impatiently; it was hard getting through work when all she wanted was to dash to MI headquarters and explain what had happened.

The voice at the other end of the line became more enthusiastic. 'Hold on, Miss Marissa. Dr. Max will talk to you in a moment.'

Sure enough, Max's deep voice came through half a minute later. Marissa paced as he went through the usual pleasantries... how are you, how was your experience, I hope there were no unpleasant side-effects, yadda yadda... when she decided that she had enough and cut through his blabber. 'Max, I need stronger pills. Whatever is in those pills, it's not enough.'

A long silence answered her. When Max finally spoke again, his tone was grim. 'That is not a good idea. The drug is calibrated according to your body mass and theoretical tolerance —'

'It's not bloody enough!' Marissa snapped. Tears sprang to her eyes and she choked. 'I... I was reliving the play date that I had with Vanessa, back when we were kids, but then these present-day thoughts intruded and... Look, I signed up for this so that I could fully immerse myself in my past... actually relive it, not just recall memories.'

'I understand, but —'

'I don't want to feel it consciously as a memory, okay?! You promised me it would be just like a dream, only more real!'

Max sounded alarmed. He mentally calculated the number of pills still in Marissa's possession — four remaining pills, if she had followed the schedule, and began to worry. 'Calm down, Marissa. Okay, maybe we can increase the dosage by a tiny bit. That should help you without significantly damaging your health. Why don't you drop by tomorrow and we'll discuss this further? We might have to do some tests on you. In the meantime, try to take another pill tonight ya? Just one, as recommended.'

Marissa let out a small sob, but she agreed. Max thought of telling her to stop altogether, but he worried that it might backfire, so the best course of action was to let her take her usual dosage. 'Do not, I repeat, *do not* take more than one pill, you understand? We will get this sorted out, but only if you follow my instructions.'

Yes, you need to calm down, Marissa chided herself. After all, Max had already told her that the pills were still in the experimental stage, so they had to play it safe. Plus, what she was getting from the pills was definitely more immersive than sitting in her room remembering the good times she had with Vanessa; she could swear that she could feel the touch of her hand and hear her laughter.

She hung up after they ironed out the details of the meeting. She even apologised to Max for her emotional outburst, to Max's relief. Marissa sat down on her bed, head hung low. It had been eight months since Vanessa died, but every day since then she thought about her. More so than when she was alive, and it was this realisation that caused her pain. Their parents and Thomas, their brother, seemed to have moved on with life, but Marissa refused to because it was *unfair*.

It was supposed to be a good day for Vanessa; she was on her way to a gathering with friends, and she had put on her best dress. Before she left, she even promised Marissa that she would buy some fries for her on the way back. Vanessa never reached her destination, her journey cut short when a douchebag, on the phone while driving, drifted into her lane. Vanessa swerved to her left, and into the path of a truck.

I could have torn that bastard into pieces, Marissa thought. Tears fell onto the framed photo of her sister on her lap. The worst thing about death is its finality. There are no more chances, no last goodbyes. Vanessa and her pretend-perfect were gone.

Slowly, her gaze went to the small bottle of white pills beside her bed. With grim determination, she swallowed a pill, lay down on her bed and pulled the blanket over her body.

Marissa giggled as Vanessa grinned conspiratorially. They were not allowed to eat junk food, but Vanessa managed to smuggle a packet of cheese flavoured potato chips that she bought from a stall outside her school. Seated on the edge of their shared bed, legs dangling over the side, they devoured the chips greedily.

'I feel bad for Thomas. We never let him have any of these chips,' Marissa commented.

'We can't let him join us,' Vanessa replied. 'He always tells Mum.'

Once they were done, Vanessa folded the plastic bag into a small square — she had a methodical way of folding it — and stuffed it into one of the small pockets of her school bag. 'Make sure you wash your hands with soap. We can't risk Mum smelling them.'

Marissa brought her hand to her nose, and sure enough, the smell of grease and artificial cheese was discernible. When she blinked, they were now in the car instead.

Why does this keep happening? There aren't supposed to be any breaks in continuity.

Slowly, Marissa's view of the car began to fade, and she felt herself getting pulled out of that past immersion.

NO! She resisted with all her might, focusing on the interior of the car. Back then, their father had driven a second-hand Honda. Music was drifting from the radio. It was one of Michael Jackson's older songs, and to her right Vanessa, appearing to be around fifteen years old, was staring out of the window. When she turned to face Marissa, she looked bored. 'Let's play a game,' she suggested.

'What game?'

'Hmm... how about this? We pick a category, like song titles or famous people or something, and then we come up with an example for each letter of the alphabet. For example, for singers we have A for ABBA, B for Bee Gees, and so on.'

I have no idea how Vanessa came up with such games. We used to pass the time on a lot of car trips playing nonsensical games to entertain ourselves, some more fun than others. Sometimes Mum and Dad and Thomas joined in, as in the case of this game.

'We start with countries,' Vanessa decided. 'A for Andorra.'

Andorra. I still have no idea where that place is.

Marissa blinked. The twelve-year-old Marissa had the general knowledge of a teapot, and she struggled to come up with something. From the front of the car their father added, 'Angola.'

'B for Brazil,' Vanessa continued effortlessly. 'C for Congo, D for Denmark, E for Estonia, F for Finland...' Vanessa's voice grew increasingly distorted, and Marissa could no longer make out the words.

Stop! Please, let me stay in this immersion!

Her best efforts to remain in that Revisit session ended in disappointment. When Marissa opened her eyes, she could not see anything. The inky darkness of the night enveloped her. Her memory seemed unreliable, her reality unsteady. Only one word rang in her mind: Zimbabwe.

The pill I took tonight isn't working, she thought. She lay there on the bed and stared at the ceiling, disappointed. As far as her Revisit sessions went, this was terrible, insubstantial. Oddly resigned to her fate, she closed her eyes again and waited for dawn to come.

Dr. Max gestured at the chair as he typed something into the computer. 'Have a seat, Marissa. We'll do the usual tests, as agreed.'

Marissa took a deep breath and settled down. Immediately, the nurses appeared. One of them took some blood samples and disappeared into the adjoining room. Later, Marissa gave them a urine sample and had her eyes checked. It was all pretty routine by now.

'We have to make sure that your kidneys and liver aren't deteriorating,' Max explained. He took her hands and examined her nails. 'How were the sessions?'

Marissa explained how the latest sessions went, describing the discontinuities and the random, self-aware thoughts that popped into her head. Max nodded gravely. 'We will need to run some tests for confirmation, but I am afraid that your body is getting used to the drugs. That's why the effects are waning, and you are experiencing erratic jumps in the sessions.'

'Give me a higher dosage,' Marissa said firmly.

There was reluctance written all over Max's face. 'We have prepared a new batch of pills for you, but in the end, we will stop this trial if your health is compromised, understood? Also, with the higher dosage, you now have to let 48 hours pass between pills.'

Marissa nodded, although she knew that even at the expense of her health, she would still go ahead with the pills just to see Vanessa again. It was all that mattered right now.

The stronger pills worked, and Marissa returned to being a functioning adult. She found her focus and her motivation again. Work went well, she reconnected with some of her friends, and she even signed up for yoga classes. She gleefully ignored Max's warning about having a 48-hour break between the pills as she felt no ill effects.

Marissa woke up one day from her Revisit experience with a bad case of sore throat. She dismissed it as due to not drinking enough water. When she stepped onto the floor, a sharp pain shot up her legs. She looked down and saw that the skin on her heels was badly cracked and bloody. That dampened her day even before it started. To make matters worse, she had to walk around a lot that day at work, and her wounds hurt with every step. She briefly debated calling Max, but she decided against alarming him, or worse, him stopping the supply of pills.

Still, there was the next Revisit session awaiting her. That gave her the strength to get through the day.

Her skin got drier. She practically slathered herself with bottles of moisturisers, but that seemed to be only a temporary solution. Drinking lots of water did not help either. The voice of reason in her head told her to stop taking the pills and to call Max, but she looked at the bottle and saw three remaining pills and decided that she could afford to wait three more days. After all, why bother making another trip to MI when she would be there in a few days to get her refills anyway?

The sessions were beginning to feel less immersive again. For the past few nights, she frequently found the intrusion of her conscious thoughts, and the illusion was quickly dispelled. Still, the interruptions were nowhere as bad as with the previous batch of pills.

That night, the memory she revisited was that of the day Vanessa died. They were sitting at the dining table, having pancakes that Vanessa, in a wave of enthusiasm, had made. 'They are kind of burnt, but put more honey and butter on them and you probably won't notice it,' she said.

Marissa rolled her eyes, but took the pancakes anyway. Vanessa might not be a fantastic cook, but pancakes are pancakes and she was hungry. 'What time are you going out to meet your friends?'

'Around noon. Well, you know how they are like, perpetually late, and the usual excuse about traffic jams. It's like they don't know it will be congested,' Vanessa complained with a shake of her head.

'Pot calling the kettle black,' Marissa said with a smile.

'Hey, I am only tardy when I am with tardy people! Just shut up and eat your pancakes.'

Was she running late? Was that why she was speeding? She was going at 140 km per hour when the accident happened. Could it have been averted if she had just left the house earlier?

Just like that, Marissa found herself in bed, heart racing. For a few minutes, she was disoriented from the instant jump between the world of her memories and the present. 'Vanessa... I should have stopped her,' she said softly to herself. Tears streamed down the sides of her face.

Her grief was soon replaced by anger. It was the last memory she had of Vanessa, and her reliving it was interrupted. She clenched her fists as she sobbed. That was a very precious memory, and her conscious thoughts just had to ruin it. She remembered how Vanessa threw one last look at her, her blue dress swishing around her, and gave her a little wave as she closed the door behind her. I didn't even get to reach that part, Marissa thought.

. . . The Universe Splits . . .

Propelled by her rage, she grabbed the bottle beside her and unscrewed the cap. She popped the two remaining pills into her mouth and lay down. I don't care what happens anymore, she told herself. I need to relive that moment, this time fully. No interruptions, no discontinuities.

Vanessa was wearing her blue dress, but she made no effort to leave. Sitting on the sofa in their living room, the two sisters were engrossed in a game of Scrabble. 'I am feeling a little lazy to go out now,' Vanessa said, checking her watch. 'I am very late anyway. I will just call my friends and tell them I won't be joining them after all.'

Marissa gave her a playful jab on the arm. 'Bad friend, but I am sure they will understand. It is not the first time you have ditched them.'

'Shush...' Vanessa dialled one of her friends' numbers. 'Hey Jenny... sorry, I don't think I can make it after all. I am having period pains and it's getting worse, so I think I'll skip this.' There was a brief silence as Jenny said something, after which Vanessa said, 'Yup, I will just curl up into a ball and wish I was a man instead. Thanks, Jenny. You guys have fun, and send me pictures okay?'

Once Vanessa hung up, she grinned conspiratorially and nudged Marissa. 'Come on, your turn. Put out something so that I can destroy you with my awesome word.'

Marissa looked at her letters, and asked innocently, 'Is "Fende" a brand or a word?'

'That's not a valid word, silly,' Vanessa answered with a laugh. Marissa laughed too, and thought that Vanessa's laughter was more precious than anything.

Max stared at the picture. If it wasn't for the discolouration of her face, Marissa could just be sleeping. Technically, she was sleeping, he thought. With a sigh, he moved the picture away and focused on the autopsy report instead. As expected, her liver and kidneys were in bad shape, but it was her heart that had failed first. He checked the intake schedule that he had planned for her, and concluded that Marissa had ignored his warnings. She overdosed, plain and simple.

The pills were a drug after all, he mused, but the real drug was the precious memories these subjects held on to. In their depressed state, those memories were all they had. Max had bought into the idea that these pills could help people with depression, anxiety disorders and post-traumatic stress disorder, but it was probably not a good idea to let them skip counselling altogether. Like Marissa, he thought ruefully.

Dr. Sophie Mendez came into his office and gestured towards the folder on his desk. 'I saw the report. It's... tragic. I think it was a mistake giving her a higher dose.'

'To be honest, it probably wouldn't have mattered,' Max said, in a matter-of-fact tone. 'The subjects can still OD from the pills, even if we give them the basic dosage, if they insist on finishing the whole bottle at once.'

'Then we probably shouldn't give them more than three pills in one go,' Sophie replied. She sighed. 'Well, I hope she died with happy memories.'

Max rearranged the stack of reports, placed Marissa's picture back into the folder, and stowed it away in the cabinet. 'We can be sure that she did.'

Meanwhile . . .

... in an Alternative Universe ...

She reached for the bottle of pills, but in the process knocked over the framed picture of Vanessa. The ensuing crash and the shattering of glass cut through the silence of the night. Marissa sat stunned in her bed, staring at the broken frame.

As she continued to stare at the broken pieces on the floor, the realisation finally arose with sharp clarity in her consciousness: Vanessa was gone, and she was never coming back; that was an immutable fact. The one person she could relate to, to talk to and to hang out with, had been taken away from her a long time ago. But her own time on this earth had stopped along with Vanessa's; she was still alive, but she had not been living for the past eight months.

There was the sound of hurried footsteps, and moments later the door flung open and the faces of her worried family members appeared. 'Marissa, are you alright? What was that noise?' her mother asked. Her question was answered when they followed her line of sight to the mess on the floor.

'I'll get the broom,' her father announced gruffly. Thomas remained rooted at the entrance to Marissa's room, watching with bleary eyes.

Her mother sat down on the bed. Noticing the puffy eyes and the tear stains on Marissa's cheeks, she took her daughter's hand and calmly said, 'Marissa, you need to let Vanessa go.'

Marissa snatched her hand away. 'Like you all did? How could you move on just like that? Didn't she mean anything to you? How could you —'

'Stop acting like you were the only one who mourned for her. She was my sister too,' Thomas snapped from the doorway.

'SHUT UP! You were gallivanting around Europe a month after she died!' Marissa yelled. She then turned to her mother. 'And you! You would have cleared her room out if I hadn't stopped you! I was the one who picked her belongings from the dustbin... and her dresses...' The tears came again, and she was powerless to stop them. 'I tried so hard to preserve the memory of her, but none of you seemed to care.'

Thomas rolled his eyes. 'Oh, stuff it, Marissa. I went to Europe because that was how I coped with her death. You think it was easy for me to look at our driveway and re-member the last time she drove out of it?' He began to cry as well. 'I know that you were especially close to her, and that I was unwanted in the little clique the two of you formed, but I've lost one sister and I feel like I've lost you too!'

Marissa watched Thomas storm off, shocked. She had never considered how everyone else around her had felt. It was true that she was closest to Vanessa, but Vanessa was a sister and a daughter to them too. She realised that her self-centeredness had blinded her to the grief of her family.

'We all did. We all felt like we lost you too,' her mother said softly before retreating into her own room.

As her father wordlessly swept the broken glass away, Marissa watched him. How he had aged, she thought. It struck her that instead of spending time with her parents, she had neglected them, and when they too passed away one day, what then? More pills to cope with her loss?

She stood up, walked to her father just as he was done cleaning up, and hugged him. He returned her embrace and wept.

'I wish it had worked,' Max said, as he checked Marissa's blood pressure.

'It would have been great if it did, but I would like to move on,' Marissa replied. 'I have made an appointment with a psychiatrist now, and I have my family's support... well, it won't be easy, but I think I will be all right.'

Max nodded. 'If you need any advice, feel free to call me. That was dangerous though, ignoring my orders. You could have died. Your kidneys and liver were not doing so great, although if you continue with the medication I prescribed, the damage should be undone, or at least, contained.' He then reached for the form on the tray beside him and handed it to Marissa. 'So, by signing this form, you are officially off this Memory Inc. programme, although you are advised to return for a check-up every month or so.'

Marissa studied the form in her hand, and she glanced at the bottle with the remaining two pills now sitting on Max's desk. She recalled how close she had come to consuming them all at one go. If she hadn't knocked over Vanessa's photo, she probably would have died. Without any hesitation, she signed the form and returned it to Max.

'I wish you all the best,' Max said, offering his hand.

'Thank you,' she replied as she shook Max's hand.

As she stepped out of the building, she took a deep breath. This new beginning of hers felt frightening, unpredictable and unsteady. It was the same feeling she had had when she was pounded by the waves on the beach back as a kid. She no longer had Vanessa to assuage her fears or hold her hand — but she was keen to move forward.

After all, the time for her to stand on her own was long overdue.

SORRY, NOT SORRY

MH

'Sorry.'

One word can carry so much meaning. It can mend broken relationships and soothe pained hearts.

It is also the one word I don't believe in. To me, that word is pointless, a pathetic attempt to right what is wrong. To rid yourself of guilt. People get careless with their words and their actions because they think that saying 'sorry' nullifies whatever harm they have caused.

'Stuck in a meeting; boss just wouldn't shut up.' Nigel flashes me one of his charming smiles in an attempt to boost the power of his apology. I remain unfazed, and mentally scoff at it. Nigel has been stuck in meetings and doing important things that justify his lack of punctuality since he was twelve.

He takes the seat opposite mine, and motions for the waitress. I study him as he orders an espresso. He is clean-shaven and is wearing a well-made suit with a silk tie and cufflinks. Typical Nigel; he never lets anyone forget that he is an accomplished manager. Me, I have always been a T-shirt and baggy pants kind of girl, with, according to my mother at least, questionable tastes.

Just looking at Nigel annoys me because he reminds me of how far I have fallen behind in life. I resent him for that.

'How was culinary school? It would be an honour to taste the food you cook,' he asks in an attempt to dispel the awkward silence that has settled between us.

I reply with a shrug and mumble, 'It's alright. I like it.' Right away, I get down to business. After all, it's not like we have a lot to talk about. I reach into my backpack and hand over a nicely wrapped package. 'My mother got this for your Mum. Something from Brisbane.'

Our relationship wasn't always this strained. We are cousins; our mothers, sisters. I spent a significant portion of my childhood with Nigel and his brothers, but it was Nigel that I adored and admired the most twenty plus years ago. There was a time when he was my idol, and even then, he could get people to do anything he wanted. Some people are just born with charisma, I suppose. Now he is the successful manager of a construction company, and I am a cook. He earns in a month what I earn in half a year, and I am not surprised; he was destined for success, from his birth into an affluent family to a superior education system designed to bring out the best in a student.

In contrast, I lost the lottery called life. While Nigel's mother married an up-and-rising engineer, mine married a compulsive gambler who disappeared with a hefty debt to his name. While Nigel did his homework under the guidance of attentive tutors, I was wondering if I would ever go to school again. Then, just as things were bad enough, Nigel knocked me further down in life, on one fateful afternoon.

'We aren't supposed to play on this side of the room!' I protested, ever the obedient child.

Nigel, ten at that time, stuck out his tongue at me. 'Catch me if you can.'

'It's not fair!' I warily eyed the rows and rows of expensive, fragile memorabilia on the display shelf. Those were Aunt Margaret's treasures, and Nigel knew the rules: no running or playing in this area. Yet every time he sensed he was losing in our game of tag, he would run there. What a cheat.

'I'll count to ten, and if you don't come in time, you lose!' he jeered.

Heart thumping, I wondered if it was worth breaking the rules that Aunt Margaret set for us. Nigel would get away with it since he was her son, but me? When Aunt Margaret agreed to let us stay in their spacious bungalow, she gave us daily reminders that the welcome was not unconditional.

Nigel started counting. Even as Aunt Margaret's warning played in my head, I was adamant not to let him win again by hiding in the forbidden area, so I took two steps forward. He was shocked that I answered his dare, and in his haste, he bumped against the shelf.

Both of us gasped in horror. We watched as the porcelain Buddha statue tumbled off the shelf. It fell in what seemed like slow motion to my eight year-old self, and Nigel desperately tried to reach for it in mid-air, but alas, what we got instead was a loud crash and hundreds of porcelain shards. Worse, the impact cracked a floor tile.

Aunt Margaret appeared immediately, followed meekly by my mother, their preparations for dinner abandoned. They were livid.

'It was Carrie's fault!' Nigel cried out accusingly.

I froze. In my shock, I suppose I looked guilty. 'No, I —'

Before I could finish, my mother was right in front of me. She was not there to comfort or even to question me, but to deliver a stinging slap to my face.

'It wasn't me!' I blurted out. I cradled my cheek, hot tears running down my face.

Nigel's voice was shaky, but I heard him say, 'I told her not to play near this area, but she wouldn't listen!'

My hand dropped. 'That's not true!' I screamed. My left cheek burned more with humiliation than pain, and at that moment all I could think of was how I wished Nigel would get his comeuppance. I could have punched him, or scratched his face bloody. Instead, what I got was a sharp rap on my head.

'Say you are sorry, Carrie,' my mother snapped.

Adamantly, I shook my head. 'IT WASN'T ME!'

My mother's index finger and thumb twisted the flesh on my arm so hard that I thought she was going to rip off a chunk. Margaret only watched silently, too distraught over the loss of her precious Buddha statue to say anything. I channelled all my hatred for Nigel when I glanced at him; he was scared, but I could tell he was glad I was the one being punished for his misdeed.

Another slap landed on my other cheek. 'Just say sorry, you stupid girl!' Mum cried out. Her face was red, and her eyes showed desperation. 'Aunt Margaret has been so kind to let us stay with her ever since your useless father left us! The least you can do is to say you're sorry!'

There it was again, the 'they let us stay with them, so we are at their mercy' logic. I hated it. It was despicable. You'd think that if your sister and her daughter were at risk of having to live under a bridge, the least you could do was to give them shelter until they were back on their feet, but no, it was as if we had signed our souls over the moment we stepped into this house.

I shook my head obstinately. 'Sorry' was a word you use when you are guilty, and I was not. Plus, I hated the debt of gratitude we found ourselves in, so I was determined not to let them bully me into confessing. 'It was Nigel who bumped against the shelf!' I yelled as my mother spanked me.

'Don't lie, Carrie!' Mum roared. In her desperation, she delivered a hard slap to the left side of my head that sent me reeling.

Pain erupted. I touched my injured face. By the time the burn on my cheek dissipated, I realised that I could no longer hear through my left ear.

'The surgery will fix your hearing. There is nothing to be afraid of,' Mum said, more to reassure herself than me.

I let her hold my hand as I lay in the hospital bed, but an unbridgeable gap had already opened between us. My love for my mother had died; she chose to trust Nigel over me, her only daughter. All we had was each other, and she betrayed me. I could no longer trust Nigel either; my respect for him evaporated together with the tears in my eyes.

'We don't have to go back to that house anymore. I have found an apartment we can rent, and I got a job washing dishes in a school canteen. We will be alright,' Mum said. She gave my hand a squeeze. It was a gesture I did not reciprocate as I kept my eyes trained on the ceiling. 'Carrie, I am so sorry. Will you forgive Mummy?'

I pulled my hand out of hers. Since I could no longer hear out of my left ear, I found that by lying on my right side and pressing my ear against the pillow, I could block out any sound. I squeezed my eyes shut and did just that.

Nigel offers to pay for our meals because it is another chance for him to make a good impression and show off how rich he is. I am dying to get away from him, because every time I look at him, I am reminded of his expression when my mother took her frustration and her fear out on me: pale, frightened but glad at the same time. I remember how his lips clammed up when I was praying for him to say something. Ironically, I can't get him to shut up now.

'Remember how we used to cycle to the nearby shops to buy soft drinks? Our mothers didn't let us drink them, so we would steal out and finish everything by the drain around the field,' Nigel reminisces.

Ah, the good old days. I nod, but I find myself unable to add anything to the conversation. Instead, I keep my eyes on the ground. I am now fascinated by how his shoelaces, which had come undone a few minutes ago, dance and slap the pavement with every step.

We are now walking towards his new house, where he stays with his mother. For some reason, I felt compelled to accept his invitation despite my reluctance to see Aunt Margaret again. It might have something to do with the fact that the house is not far from where we were, and I thought that if I humoured him this time, perhaps he would leave me alone in the future.

'We used to have duels with the plastic swords my Mum bought for us, remember? Yours was purple and mine was green,' he continues.

'Yes.' I feel sweat roll down the sides of my face, and I look around. We are making our way through a park, deserted under the harsh midday sun, and Nigel's voice seems to echo in this space. I glance at him, see the blissful expression on his face, and lower my gaze again. At least the shoelaces do not offend me the way his face does.

Nigel keeps going on despite my silence. He doesn't seem to get the hint. 'Hey, listen. I guess we drifted apart, ya?' he says, placing a hand on my shoulder.

I flinch. He looks a little hurt at my reaction; rejection is a concept foreign to him. 'I keep thinking about that incident when we were kids, and I am so sorry. It has haunted me for years. I am so glad you did not suffer permanent hearing loss.' He gestures at my ear. 'Your hearing... it's okay now, right?'

'Yes.'

Truth be told, I am convinced that the hearing in my left ear is inferior, despite tests saying otherwise. Doctors think it could be psychological, a result of the trauma I suffered. But it wasn't just the hearing. That event transformed me. It turned me away from my mother, and over the years, I found myself struggling to maintain friendships and romantic relationships. My inability to trust people, to say sorry and to forgive people, means that I burn bridges faster than I can build them. I had a hard time fitting in and barely managed to graduate from high school. At no point in time did I feel like I was in control of my life.

You will never know how important the word 'sorry' is until you can't say it.

'Oh, well, I need to say it again. Sorry, Carrie, for what happened. I couldn't sleep well for weeks. It was unfortunate, and I wish I could turn back time to stop your mother from slapping you,' he says with all the earnestness he can muster.

He takes a few steps forward, while I remain rooted at my spot. My entire life, ruined, and he thinks he can fix it with a single word. What a fucking joke. And instead of just stopping my mother from hitting me, why not go back in time to confess? Does he truly feel responsible for what happened?

'I still have trouble sleeping now,' I blurt out. It is true; every once in a while, I dream of being slapped so hard that when I wake up I can feel my left cheek tingle. Sometimes, in a state of panic, I think that my hearing, which had been dutifully restored by doctors, has left me again. I usually end up pressing my phone to my left ear and playing the alarm repeatedly to assure myself that all is well.

Nigel looks sorry, but his expression seems fake to me. Duh, of course it is. He is glad that our fortunes were not reversed, that I was the one who suffered a setback while he marched towards success. 'Sorry to hear that, Carrie.' He looks ahead. 'Let's continue on our way; it's getting uncomfortably warm here. We just need to go down this flight of stairs. My house is at the end of the path.'

I clench my fists, but I follow his lead without a word. He takes one step down the stairs, and I watch as his left foot lands on the shoelace. Moments later, he lets out a yelp as he falls forward.

At that instant, my mind rewinds to that fateful day, the day the statue tumbled through the air and smashed into countless pieces. The day my life started down this wretched path.

Tears fill my eyes.

Nigel manages to regain his balance and heaves a sigh of relief. It is a steep and long way down, and there is little doubt that he would have broken something had he fallen.

. . . The Universe Splits . . .

108

He looks at me and grins sheepishly. 'That was a close one!'

I blink away the tears and force myself to smile. 'Nigel?'

He bends down, his fingers around his shoelace. 'What?'

'I'm sorry.'

And with that, I press my palms onto his back and throw my entire weight into the shove. All those years of pain, resentment and crushed dreams go into that single push.

I watch him fall for a long time, tumbling and rolling, head over heels. As he reaches the bottom, I hear a crack, although given the distance, it is possible that it was just my imagination.

But the buoyant feeling in me is unmistakable. A smile creeps up my lips. It feels like I have my life under control again. All with that single push.

Moments pass. I take a deep breath and run down the flight of stairs towards Nigel's twisted body. I scream for help because that feels like the right thing to do. The area is deserted, so echoes answer my cries. By the time I finally get to the bottom, I am out of breath. Yet, I must admit, I have never felt more alive.

I kneel beside Nigel's body. His face is pointing away from me, and his legs are twisted at an unnatural angle under him. I feel for a pulse, but there is nothing.

'I am sorry,' I say one more time.

But of course, I don't mean it.

Meanwhile . . .

109

He looks at me and grins sheepishly. 'That was a close one!'

I am suddenly fixated on the thought of him falling. The image of the Buddha statue tumbling through thin air is superimposed with the image of Nigel experiencing the same fate, porcelain and flesh matching each other turn by turn before finally breaking into hundreds of pieces. Primal forces surge in me... my life could change this very moment... all it would take is a push, and I would have my sweet revenge —

And then what? My analytical brain intervenes. Pushing Nigel will not turn back time and undo all the hurt. What I have, my anxiety, my strained relationship with my mother, my relatively low standing in life, will remain. They had come to define me, and I let them.

Nigel waves a hand over my face. 'Carrie? Are you alright?'

I blink and shake my head. Suddenly I feel very tired; everything feels pointless. For what purpose have I carried the hate accumulated from the years of being bitter? 'I'm sorry, I don't think I can go on,' I say, no longer willing to be anywhere near Nigel or visit his house. I turn around sharply, and as Nigel calls out my name, I break into a run, the ground a blurry patch through my tears.

Throughout my life, there were plenty of things I had wished for. I wish my father had not left us. I wish my mother and I had not found ourselves destitute and reliant on Nigel's family. I wish Mum had believed in me and not slapped me. I wish I had done better in school. All futile wishes; I cannot change my past. But there is still one wish that I tend to overlook: my wish to be happy.

Maybe I should work on that.

I wish I could say that everything in my life is awesome now, but that is not true. It is taking quite a bit of effort to put my past behind me. The burden certainly feels lighter though, now that I no longer hold on to all the hatred and the pessimism. My relationship with my mother has also improved; it took me three days to gather the courage to offer her the olive branch and a week-long trip to Spain for the both of us to dispel the awkwardness that had settled between us. The trip wiped out half of my very meagre savings, but it was worth it.

Sometimes I return to my bitter, cynical self. I get mean and snap at people. Like I said, it takes time and effort, so I forgive myself when I suffer a relapse. It helps that I have learnt to apologise sincerely too. I understand now why 'sorry' is needed in our vocabulary: it isn't so that people can afford to be careless and hurt others, but because humans are imperfect and short-sighted creatures. We make mistakes, and sometimes we don't see the consequence of our actions until it is too late. Time is a cruel master, unrelenting in its march forward, so all we can do is to forgive each other. My younger self would have scoffed at such pretentious drivel, but I quite like my current approach to it.

I avoid Nigel's attempts to contact me; better not to push my tolerance, huh? The less I think of him, the less I allow the childhood incident to define me. The nightmares about losing my hearing are still there, but they are less intense and less frequent now. I'd like to think of it as a sign of my recovery. If Nigel still feels guilty, well, the burden is for him to bear.

Am I truly happy now? That depends, really. There are good days and bad days, but overall there are more of the former, and that's enough for me. I am still a struggling cook, but I hope I can move on to something better in the future.

Hope. There is always hope.

THE BYSTANDER

YK

Bus 19 was always late. Every morning I had to spend about fifteen to twenty minutes just waiting at the bus stop. Fifteen at least. For five days a week, that added up to seventy-five minutes spent just waiting at the bus stop.

That's plenty of time to spend with a few strangers also waiting for Bus 19. So, even though I had never spoken a single word to any of them, it felt like I knew them extremely well. The strangers didn't seem like strangers anymore. They had become a familiar presence.

There was a woman, probably in her late forties or early fifties, who carried a lot of stuff with her. She had short hair and was always dressed in a blue polo T-shirt with some company logo above the pocket, clearly her work uniform. There was also an old man wearing thick glasses who only wore different variations of loose shirts and slacks. He carried nothing but a plastic bag that smelled of food. Occasionally the old man and the woman would casually talk to each other, but on most days they just sat in silence and kept to themselves, barely acknowledging the other's presence. I guess those two people had been taking Bus 19 for years and exchanged kind pleasantries every now and then.

And then there was Logan. That was not his real name, but just a name I gave him because he looked like a 'Logan'. The first time I saw him, he looked handsome and dapper in ridiculously formal clothes. To a single woman in her mid-twenties like me, people like Logan stood out, though he took no notice of me in my frumpy skirt and cardigan. That day, he was clearly going for a job interview, since a few days later he started wearing slightly less formal work clothes and took Bus 19 regularly with the rest of us.

He seemed like a kind and friendly person. Once he helped the woman with the blue polo-T carry her things. After the ice had been broken between them, the lady and Logan struck up a conversation. It was mostly idle chatter about the weather, traffic, and how that damn Bus 19 was always late. So, what I gathered about Logan at that time was that he was handsome, gentle and friendly. As a single woman in her mid-twenties, I took notice of that too.

At one point the woman asked him where he lived, and he looked down the street and said, 'Right there, second house after the turn.'

I was so caught up eavesdropping on their conversation that I turned to look at where he was pointing and he noticed! He looked at me for half a second before resuming his conversation with the lady. I felt so embarrassed that I could feel my face turning hot as my stomach churned.

The days passed by, and everyone seemed to settle into their routines. The old man with his bag of food, the woman in her work uniform, and Logan, usually sitting at the side looking at his phone. I wished I had the courage to strike up a conversation with him, but I was too shy to do so.

When the bus eventually arrived, it was usually fairly crowded. He got off at a stop where all the tech start-ups and R&D companies were found. I guessed that he was either working as an entrepreneur or was a scientist of some sort. That meant he was smart too.

The street where he lived was between my house and the bus stop. So, I started walking by that street every morning on my way to the bus stop. His was a small but cosy single-storey house, and it looked clean and tidy. I caught a glimpse of exercise equipment through an open window. Sometimes he came out of his house just as I walked by, and ended up walking either behind or in front of me towards the stop. He always sat in the same spot at the bus stop, taking out his phone and looking at it until the bus arrived.

I noticed him staring at me one day, when the weather was hot and I was in a particularly revealing summer dress. We made eye contact and he smiled. I tried to smile back, but it probably ended up looking like I twitched my mouth, so I hurriedly looked away. He resumed looking at his phone. *So, that's what it takes for him to notice me?* A few more days went by. He never talked to me, nor did I try to chat him up either.

One day, when the bus was especially late, he seemed different. I saw him smiling as he texted on his phone. I wondered to whom he could be texting to. It could only be his girlfriend, or someone who was about to be, I thought with a slight tinge of jealousy. He was not married since there was no ring on his finger — I looked. By the next morning, it couldn't be more obvious. He came to the bus stop with a woman, all laughing and giggling as they waited for the bus. Her hair looked slightly dishevelled as she kept trying to comb it between doses of breath spray sent into her mouth. Her blouse was wrinkled at places and needed ironing. It didn't require a genius to conclude that she had spent the night at his place, and was now heading to work without much time to shower or freshen up.

When the bus came, Logan remained seated next to the woman.

'Your bus is here! Go!' she said.

'No. I'll spend a few more minutes with you until your bus comes,' he replied.

The polo-T woman, the old man, and I got on Bus 19, while he stayed behind with his girlfriend.

For the next few days, she was with him at the bus stop. Though on some days neither of them was there. Presumably, that's when Logan was at her place. When I came back from work at night, I could see them walking together near his house.

Within two months, they had settled into a new routine. She had moved in with him and every morning they came to the bus stop together. She took bus 42, which usually came before Bus 19. They kissed each other goodbye as she got on 42, then he returned to his usual spot and took out his phone.

'It's okay, you don't need to work,' he said one morning to his girlfriend, 'I make enough to support both of us.'

'That's nice, but I need something to do. I can't just stay at home the whole day,' she protested.

'You can do whatever you want,' he said, 'you could work on your sculpting. Make stuff. Or, you said you like cooking, right? I love your cooking!'

'You're just trying to convince me to stay at home and cook you dinner every day.'

He laughed, gave her a kiss, and said, 'Baby, you can do whatever you want.'

I figured that the woman had quit her job since she no longer took her own bus to work anymore. At most, she accompanied Logan to the bus stop, wearing comfortable tank or spaghetti tops with sweatpants. She wasn't dressed for work. They waited for Bus 19 together, and she saw him off when we got on the bus. She waved him goodbye as the bus drove away with the rest of us on board.

One rainy morning, I noticed that they were arguing, though they were trying not to shout and attract attention to themselves. They probably thought we couldn't hear them, since they were at the far corner of the bus stop, away from the rest of us. But it was clearly a heated argument.

'I didn't want to go in the first place,' she said.

'Yeah, you didn't. Until you went and found a bunch of guys to throw yourself at.'

'"Throw myself"? I was just talking. They were *your* friends.'

'Yeah. My friends. So why were you talking to them?'

'Since when do you decide who I get to talk to?'

'Since you became my girlfriend.'

'No,' she said, 'That's not how it works. I get to talk to whoever —'

He grabbed both of her arms tightly.

'Do you know what the guys will think of me, Clara? My girlfriend getting drunk and flirting with guys!'

'Let go, Jason,' she said, 'your bus is here.'

That was the point when the rain seemed to also fall on the picture I had painted in my head; the water dissolving the image of a handsome, friendly, kind, athletic, attractive man, slowly revealing the reality underneath.

Weeks and months passed by. Jason and Clara swung between the two extremes of being happy and sweet to each other at the bus stop, to quarrelling and saying horrible things to each other. But most commonly, they just stood quietly at the bus stop, not saying much. Sometimes, the swings occurred within the same day, arriving at the bus stop happily laughing, but becoming quiet, with dark faces by the time our bus arrived. The first couple of times I saw an argument break out, she left the bus stop and headed home. Later, she just stayed there with him even after they had an argument, quietly waiting until the bus arrived, then silently waving him goodbye as we got on the bus.

I could never tell what caused their rapid mood swings, though Clara's reactions suggested that she thought she had said something wrong. One day I noticed Jason ignoring her and refusing to look away from his phone, with Clara standing behind him looking like a sad puppy. A few times she touched his arm, trying to get his attention, but he just ignored her as if she was invisible. Then I saw her taking out a phone to send a text. An instant later Jason put away his phone but continued to ignore her.

During one of the days when Clara and Jason were just sitting quietly at the bus stop, I noticed something different. They were fighting again, but Clara seemed to be acting a bit strange. I noticed that she kept tilting her head to one side, letting her hair fall over the side of her face, so I couldn't see it. My stomach tightened as I realised why. She had let her hair down so that she could cover a bruise just under her left eye.

I felt a surge of adrenaline run through my body, and my pulse quickened. Even though everyone was standing or waiting uneventfully at the bus stop, the weight of seeing the bruise on her eye came crashing down and ignited a state of alarm in my body. Suddenly I felt terrified and worried that Jason might have realised that I noticed the bruise on Clara. I tried not to move and pretended to stare absently down the street.

I took a deep breath to calm myself down and tried to think. Maybe I was over-thinking things. Maybe the bruise was due to an accident, like she fell while climbing a ladder or something. Wasn't Jason a nice and charming person who had been kind to the polo-T lady? Even I was attracted to him once, wasn't I? It was impossible that someone like him would do that to Clara. Eventually, I managed to push the thought away.

Bus 19 finally arrived, and Clara kissed Jason goodbye. Just before we got on, a weak, old man got his walker stuck against the bus door as he tried to alight. Jason was the first to rush forward to help him.

The old man thanked Jason profusely.

A few days went by, and I noticed that Clara began to dress differently. She started wearing long-sleeved sweaters and cardigans out at the bus stop with Jason, even when the weather was hot. What happened to her tank tops? I started to think about her bruise again. It had since cleared up and there wasn't anything unusual on her face. They weren't talking much, and it started to hit me how different they were from the first day I saw them.

One day, I happened to be the one wearing a sleeveless tank top. The fabric was thin and it hugged my body, showing off my figure. Not that I thought I had a good figure, but Jason was so obviously ogling me that it made me uncomfortable. It was impossible for Clara not to notice. I tried to look away and pretended not to notice anything, but I couldn't help but look at Clara's sleeves.

As I got on Bus 19, I sat as far away from Jason as I could. Then I made a plan to tell my boss that I wouldn't be coming to work the next day.

My boss was fine with me taking the day off. I woke up earlier that morning and, instead of going to the bus stop, I sat on the bench at the park on the opposite side of the road. There were some trees in the way, but I had a view of the bus stop. I could see the polo-T lady and the old man, along with Clara and Jason, as usual. I watched them as they waited for the bus, and I waited along.

Bus 19 eventually came and temporarily blocked my view of them. Through the windows, I could see the polo-T lady and the old man get on. So did Jason. The bus rolled away, leaving Clara alone at the bus stop. She stood there motionless for at least a minute or two, her face deadpan. Then she adjusted her sleeves and walked down the street, but not towards Jason's house. I stood up and followed her. She went to a coffee shop nearby. I watched a while from across the street. She ordered a coffee and a croissant before sitting down alone.

I felt nervous, a small adrenaline high hitting my body as I took a deep breath and crossed the street to enter the coffee shop. I tried to be as cheerful as possible and pretended to be surprised to see her.

'Hi! You're the one who's always at the bus stop in the morning.'

'Hello,' she said, giving me a small, perfunctory smile.

I knew I wasn't going to be invited to sit with her. So, I asked if she minded if I joined her. It wasn't something I normally did when I ran into people in public, but this time I had to. For her sake — or so I told myself. She nodded, and I sat down.

'I'm Niki,' I said.

'Clara,' she said, while adjusting her sleeves, barely making eye contact with me.

Then we were silent, as neither of us knew what to say next. I realised that I should have thought through my plan a little better. If I was going to help her in any way, I needed to be friends with her first. And to be friendly with her, I needed to start a conversation with her. But the only thing I knew about her was that she waited with Jason at the bus stop, which was a problem because I needed to be 'Clara's friend', and not be 'Clara and Jason's friend.' I wanted to avoid mentioning Jason at all cost.

I managed to blurt out, 'Where are you from?'

'Malacca,' she said, 'how about you?'

'I grew up here in Singapore, never went anywhere,' I said, 'and probably never will. I'm a shop assistant at Brickfields.'

As she raised her cup of coffee for a sip, her sleeve slipped up her arm a little, and I saw what I had suspected. There was a bruise on the middle of her arm. I only managed to catch a glimpse of it before she pulled down her sleeves again.

Despite the awkward start, we did talk for about half an hour. She said she was a graphic designer who first came to Singapore to work under a temporary contract. That was when she met Jason. In her words, they 'fell madly in love' with each other, and she stayed on in Singapore and eventually moved in with him. Her contract had ended and she was currently unemployed.

Our conversation was interrupted when she received a call from Jason on her phone. Without mentioning me at all, she said she was 'still at the coffee shop, and was just leaving.'

Just before we split up to go our separate ways, she said, 'I'm sorry, but can you please do me a favour?'

'Sure, what is it?'

She hesitated, as if trying to find the right words. Finally, she said, 'Next time we see each other at the bus stop, can we pretend that this never happened?'

'"This"? You mean meeting here at the coffee shop?'

'Yes. See, Jason and I are going through a rough time now. He might get jealous if he knew I was talking to people at coffee shops while he was at work.'

'Jealous? But I'm a woman!'

'Yes, but Jason knows I'm bisexual, so it's still a problem. He said he would die if I ever left him for a woman. It's worse than me leaving him for another man, which would be bad enough.'

'Okay, fine,' I said, 'I'm not interested in you in that way, don't worry about that. But let me give you my number. I suppose you could use a friend since you're new to Singapore and all.'

For the next few days, I headed out to work as usual. Just as I had promised Clara, I pretended that I didn't know her, and ignored them when they arrived at the bus stop. She didn't call or text me.

In the following week, I took another day off to meet Clara at the coffee shop. I met her four or five times like this, and it seemed like we were gradually feeling comfortable with each other to consider ourselves as genuine friends. I tried not to talk to her about Jason, but rather we chatted about each other's past relationships, our childhood, and our work. Mostly I told her my own stories, about this crush I once had on a guy who came to Brickfields, how my last relationship had ended badly, among other things.

I knew I couldn't keep meeting her like this, especially since I was running out of leave days, and I would lose my job if I kept missing work. During my last leave day of that year, I finally asked her about the bruises I had seen on her arm and face.

I was worried that she might withdraw and not say anything, but it was my last chance. I was surprised when she said that sometimes her arguments with Jason got out of control. She was quiet for a moment before she continued, 'I know you gave me your number, and I do enjoy talking and having coffee with you here. But I couldn't call you because Jason saw your name on my phone and started asking questions. I had to delete your number to make him happy.' I could see her tremble slightly, and tears began to roll down her eyes.

'He had no right to do that,' I protested, 'how can he decide who you're friends with?'

'Well, he loves me, and is afraid of losing me.' Even though they came from Clara's mouth, I could tell that those were Jason's words, not hers.

'Does he not understand that women can have friendships that are platonic?' I protested but immediately realised that I should not have approached the subject that way, as she seemed like she was about to shut down.

'He shouldn't do this to you, in any case,' I said, 'how bad does it get?'

'We have good and bad days. When he's good, he's really good, like Mr. Perfect, he treats me like a queen, keeps giving me gifts and compliments. But when he's in a bad mood he calls me names and insults me all the time. He even compared me to you once.'

'Me?'

'Yeah, you're "that girl at the bus stop". During sex, he took off my shirt and said he wished that my "tits were as big as that girl's at the bus stop". I got mad, and tried to leave the bedroom. But he wouldn't let me go, and he hit me until I agreed to sleep with him.'

Not that it should make a difference, but now I felt violated and felt I had a more personal stake in getting Clara out of the relationship. So, it was that day that we decided that we should make a safety plan for Clara. We went out to buy a disposable pre-paid phone. I told her to hide it somewhere safe where Jason wouldn't find it. She should use it to call me or the police if there were an emergency. We also bought a small duffel bag in which she kept some clothes and toiletries if she needed to leave the house in a hurry.

It would have been bad if I stopped meeting her immediately after she had told me her story. I needed to show her that I was there for her, whatever happened. So, despite running out of leave days, I continued meeting Clara at the coffee shop at least once a week. The weekdays were the only time for me to meet Clara without Jason around, so I had no choice but to skip work.

One night, around two in the morning, Clara called me from her pre-paid phone. She asked if she could stay at my place for a few days. They had gotten into another fight again, and Jason was throwing things at her, and threatening to beat and kill her. I lived in a rented apartment, so legally speaking I couldn't let her stay with me. But the landlord was hardly ever around, and I was sure I could sneak Clara in around him. So, of course, I agreed.

On Clara's third day staying in my room with me, I got a knock on the room door. I felt as if my heart stopped when I opened it to find Jason standing next to my landlord! Clara was in there with me, and her face turned pale with shock and fear.

'Niki, Mr. Lee here says that you've been letting this woman live with you in this apartment?'

'It's only temporary, she needed a place to stay —'

'She does have a place to stay. She lives with me,' Jason interjected.

The landlord turned to Jason and said, 'Are you sure you still want her to stay with you after what she did?'

'Wait,' I said, 'what did he say she did?'

'She stole his money and ran away,' my landlord replied.

'I didn't,' Clara said weakly.

'He beats her.' I said, getting heated, 'That's what she's running away from!'

'Mr. Lee told me she would make that excuse. Anyway, you're violating our contract. She can't stay here. And we need to stay out of their business.'

'It's alright, just get your things, Clara,' Jason said. Then he turned to the landlord and said, 'do you mind if I use your bathroom while she gets her things? We'll get out of your hair soon enough.'

The landlord nodded. There was nothing I could do. In the end, Clara told me not to worry as she gathered her stuff to leave. As she packed her things, I noticed that she had left her house keys on my dresser. On a whim, I picked up Clara's jacket and slipped in my phone before passing the jacket to her, desperately hoping that I had left my phone in silent mode. I knew Clara would be punished badly as soon as Jason got the chance.

As they left, I took out my laptop and logged into the FindMyPhone website. I let out a sigh of relief to see that the GPS on my phone was properly activated and I could see the blip moving slowly away from my apartment on the map. I got dressed and took Clara's house keys. I knew Clara left them there for me because she knew she would get beaten that night, and hoped that I was smart enough to pick up on that and could go over to stop him.

That was how I had the thought that I needed to know where Clara was at all times, especially tonight. I kept my eyes on the blip as it crossed the streets and headed towards the general direction of Jason's house.

But as the blip passed through the neighbourhood park, it stopped moving. I felt my stomach twist into knots as I tried to think of reasons why they had possibly stopped in the middle of the park beside a lake. Did the phone drop out of Clara's jacket? Could he have found the phone? Or, could he be doing something to her there? I realised in horror that the park was completely deserted at this time of the night. There wouldn't be any 'witnesses' if something happened there.

I wrote down the GPS coordinates on a piece of paper and ran downstairs to call the police from the nearest payphone — thank God they still had one of those near my place. As quickly and calmly as I could, I gave the coordinates and the location to the operator who answered my call, saying that a woman might be in danger. Then I hung up and ran towards the lake.

When I reached the lake, I found Jason sitting on top of Clara, who was lying face down. He was pushing her face into the ground.

'So, you want to leave me for that dyke huh?' he said, 'I'll show you what a real man feels like. You're gonna regret even looking at that bitch.'

Shit, I thought, I should have brought some kind of weapon with me. All I could do was to approach him and say, 'Jason, let her go.'

'Stay out of this,' he said, as he calmly turned to face me. With a smile, he continued, 'I'm telling the police that both of you are trying to steal my money to run away. You're the one who's going to jail.'

'They're not going to believe you.'

'They will. After they search your apartment and find ten thousand dollars in your apartment.'

'Why would anyone find ten... oh shit. You went to the bathroom.'

'Yes, and it's in a plastic bag inside the cistern,' he said.

My brain went into overdrive, and an idea came to me, 'Well, thanks for saying that. I got it all recorded now.'

His face changed. 'You're lying!' he said as he stood up from Clara and began to approach me.

Despite my whole body shivering with fear, I made a show of putting my hand into my jacket pocket, made a fist and pulled it out. My hand was shaking badly. But it was dark, so I hoped that he wouldn't notice that it was just my fist holding nothing. In my mind, I was trying to will the police into existence, hoping that they would arrive soon.

'You're lying,' he said again, and continued to approach. I put my fist back into my jacket. For a moment, I thought about running away, but I wasn't sure if he'd chase me. I couldn't leave Clara alone. I stood rooted but shaking as he got closer. When he reached, he pushed me to the ground and sat astride me. His movements were quick and efficient, like it was something he was very familiar with. I kept my fist balled up in my jacket pocket as he tried to pull it out.

As I struggled with him, a bright light suddenly flashed onto both of our faces.

'Sir, step away from the woman!' an authoritative voice called out.

Jason stopped moving and got off me.

In the darkness, I could just barely make out the image of a police officer pulling Jason away. 'Get on your knees and put your hands behind your back,' the voice ordered.

'Danny, help the other woman,' the officer told his partner as he handcuffed Jason.

I turned to see the other officer helping Clara up. My body was shaking too much for me to stand up on my own, and they had to come over to help me up too.

'It's alright, ladies,' said the officer, 'you're alright. It's over now.'

Not really.

Things like these aren't 'over' easily. But at least Clara was safe for now.

REUNION

YK

Order always turns to disorder. Mountains crumble. Trees wither. Flames die out; as will all the stars in the universe. Metal turns to rust. Hair turns grey, machines stop working. Things fall apart. Eventually, everything falls apart, no matter how hard you try. It's a basic rule that's true everywhere in the universe.

Our universe is a cosmic game that runs on two simple rules: (1) Things will fall apart, and (2) You can't change the past. Like chess, you are not allowed to undo your moves. If you make a mistake, there is no backtracking. There are no saves, no checkpoints for you to reload. Life is a permadeath run. The objective is to keep things as ordered for as long as possible. If you don't, you lose. Everyone gets one shot. Life is fair in that way.

I told myself to just suck it up and ride it out. It was only for one night, after all. No big deal. Besides, I had been putting it off for a long time, and decency demanded that I at least show up. Suck it up. Endure it. It was one of those things that I hated more than anything, and when it was over I always thought it wasn't so bad after all. So, I went into the restaurant telling myself that tomorrow I would wonder why I dreaded it so much.

Ten years ago, I would have found outings like these exciting. But these days they are chores to be endured. It's always the same. When meeting up with friends, you talk about what we are doing in our separate lives, talk about how long we haven't seen each other, and then talk about the 'good old days'.

I looked at my watch. 8:10 pm. They were late. I had been sitting at the restaurant bar for the past ten minutes without ordering anything. It was a fancy restaurant, one place I wouldn't normally associate with these group of friends I was about to meet. Back when we first knew each other in our Uni days, we were, of course, broke. Except perhaps for David whose parents were quite rich. Back then we were mostly hanging out in the cafeteria next to our dorms. Ten years later, now everyone has well-paying jobs, and I guess restaurants like these are the typical dining places. Or maybe David chose this place because this night was a special occasion, a reunion dinner, the first time in more than two years all of us were going to be together in one place. We already had a couple of 'reunions' before this and even those I found repetitive.

I seemed a bit under-dressed for the place and occasion, having come straight from the Uni. From work. I say 'work', but other people would call it 'school'. Being a doctoral candidate, you ride a thin line between the two. I checked my watch again, then my phone. 8:15 pm. No messages. I looked around the restaurant. It was getting crowded. The bar was dimly lit with muted fluorescent lights close to my face, making my pupils contract and everything other than the bar seemed that much darker. The bartender was ignoring me, going about her work, serving drinks to other people at the bar, and politely chatting with them.

I felt a hard pat on my back. More like a smack.

'Bro! What's up!'

I turned around. My eyes adjusted as they met David's wide grin.

'Hey — '

'They're still on the way, let's get a beer!'

David leaned forward on the bar towards the bartender and belted out a rehearsed line, 'Hey pretty lady, what does a guy have to do to get a beer around here?'

'What are you having?' The bartender smiled back.

'Kronenberg white,' he turned to me and asked, 'How about you?'

'The same.'

Two beers appeared in front of us. And we talked.

'How's it going, dude? Are you a professor yet?'

'No, not yet. Still doing my PhD.'

'Still in physics, right?'

'Yes. How about you? Still at the Barksdean?'

'Nah, I switched to Melvin and Smith. Better pay, fewer hours. Though I miss the Monday nights with my Barksdean buddies.'

Then Carol and Victor showed up. They used to date in our Uni days. Now they were married.

'Hey Carltor!' David exclaimed, 'Looking good!'

We exchanged hugs and greetings. David asked them to order a beer, but Carol said we should just move to the tables instead, and so we did. I picked up my beer and followed Carol and Victor. David, however, stepped outside for a minute to make a phone call.

'So, I heard you bought a new house,' I said, trying to make conversation. Falling into the groove of conversation. At that moment, I thought I could do this.

'Yes,' Vic said, 'up at Parks Avenue. Damn. It's 5 percent in this economy.'

I had no idea what he was talking about. It was a groove with jagged edges.

'Are you a doctor yet?' Carol asked.

'No, still working on it.'

'What's your thesis about?' asked Victor. People always ask this, and then immediately regret doing so. And I hate it when they ask, because whatever comes afterwards is always the same:

'You know, black holes and stuff,' I said, trying to give a non-committal answer.

'Woahhh,' Victor drawled out.

'I could never understand physics in school,' said Carol, 'that's why you're the smart one.'

The responses were always the same, a 'whoah' or that 'physics was too hard' for them. As if it wasn't hard for me. It had nothing to do with being smart. People working in the sciences are not all geniuses. Doing research is something that requires effort even for 'geniuses'. And they all assume that graduate students automatically move on to become successful professors. It can get annoying.

I know Carol and Victor were just being polite, but those remarks made me feel dismissed, like I was not in the same category of people as them. To them, my job and what I did was a novelty. Something amusing that they didn't hear about every day. I could almost read their minds: *I'll leave physics to the physicists; I need to work hard at a real job to support myself and a family.*

Luckily, David interrupted, 'Look who I found!'

'Hi guys, sorry I'm late.' It was Jessie, looking as beautiful as ever. She sat down next to me, smiling as she greeted me. I caught the scent of her perfume — or shampoo, I couldn't tell.

There was a brief silence as we looked at our menus. We talked again when the waiter had done taking our orders. Eventually, the conversation moved on to topics like Carol and Victor's new house, the economy, travelling, other countries, schools for the children, politics. I was quiet for the most part since I had nothing much to say. Sometimes I don't know much about the things they talk about, and other times I simply don't want to talk at all.

They were talking about the protests in Ethenia, and how the situation was starting to turn violent. The debate in the news those days was whether the Bordeo Alliance was justified in the use of force against the protesters since it wasn't clear if the Ethenian protesters were the one who started the violence in the first place.

David argued it was justified. He had read some online articles claiming that many of the protesters were members of an organised crime group, using the protests to drum up violence. That made no sense at all, but David seemed to be convincing everyone else merely by sounding very confident about his statements. He was a natural salesman.

'It doesn't make any sense,' Jessie said, 'the gangsters will have nothing to gain from this. It will undo the fight for the independence, and the BA will crack down on them even harder.'

'Does it have to make sense with these people?' David argued, 'I heard they burned down a restaurant because they saw a BA minister eating there once. These guys are nutcases.'

'Wow, that's crazy.'

As usual, the conversation evolved into where David was the centre, and the other three appeared to be soaking up the bullshit that was coming out of him. I figured this was a common social dynamic. One only has to be charming and confident to sell stuff to people. While I usually liked David, since he was a good friend, I hated being told what to think.

The talk about Ethenia soon fizzled out. Carol gave a look to Victor, who nodded. They both smiled and held hands, then turned to us.

'We have an announcement,' said Victor.

'We're pregnant!' Carol said excitedly.

'Woah!' David exclaimed, a little too loudly. Some people at the next table glared at us.

'Congratulations!' said Jessie.

'Carltor is pregnant!' said David, still loud, 'No wonder you didn't want to order anything at the bar.'

I only smiled. I wanted to say 'congratulations', but it felt redundant right after Jessie said it.

'You made me lie to the waiter,' I said, 'I should have asked for a table for six.'

'Thought you were planning to move to Australia,' said Jessie, looking at Carol's abdomen, 'now you have some extra stuff to move.'

'Well...' Carol started, but didn't finish her sentence.

'It was kind of an accident.' said Victor. That earned a sharp look from Carol, though I don't think anyone else noticed. It only happened over a fraction of a second, then Carol turned to us and said, 'Our Australia plans are on hold. At least till the baby comes.'

'Yeah, but come on guys,' Victor said excitedly, 'I'm gonna be a dad!'

'Hear hear,' David raised his glass and drank the rest of his beer.

Mistakes pile up in the cosmic game. They are inevitable. The trick is, either to make as few mistakes as possible, or to be smart enough to turn the wrong moves into right ones.

The food arrived, and we ate. Soon afterwards Victor insisted on paying for dinner. As per our reunion tradition, there was to be a karaoke session afterwards. We left the restaurant and walked towards the karaoke bar a few blocks away. Jessie fell into step next to me.

'So, seeing anyone lately?' she asked.

'No, how about you?'

'Yeah, there's this guy...'

That stung a little, but I had to continue, 'What guy? What does he do?'

'Well, I knew him since before Uni. We only got in touch again when he moved here last year.'

'He came here to work, huh?'

'Yeah. Actually, works not far from here. So, how much longer till you finish your PhD?'

'Within the year,' I said.

It was partially a lie. I was tired of repeating how research work was quite unpredictable and you start writing your thesis only when you have enough results, or when your supervisor is satisfied with your work. People nod politely when I explain, but I can tell that they are already bored before I even finish the explanation. Now when I just say 'within the year,' people never seem to notice that I had replied the same way to the same question several years ago.

That was the extent of the conversation, as we reached the karaoke bar. The rooms could only be booked in 6-hour time slots, so we got one and settled down. It was 10 pm. The rooms were dimly lit. There was a coffee table in between the couch and the karaoke setup. The floor was covered with a cheap carpet, and the walls were lined with some soft, felt material. That was to minimise echoes, I guess.

We quickly figured out how to use the karaoke machine and queued up a long list of songs into it.

On a whim, Jessie grabbed the microphone and stood up theatrically facing a large imaginary audience, 'Ladies and gentlemen, we never broke up. We just had a 14-year vacation,' she announced.

It was a quote from the Eagles on their reunion concert.

I sat there, listening and watching them sing. David sang loudly and badly, doing the headbang and air guitars during the solos. Jessie picked duets and made Carol and Victor sing together. Carol and Jessie sang *When You Believe* as Whitney Houston and Mariah Carey.

They were having a good time. Except me. I could not join them in losing myself singing into a karaoke machine. I felt reserved, as if in the company of strangers. Then it occurred to me. That was exactly what they had become. We had all changed. Of course. Graduating from university and taking on adult responsibilities does that to you. The problem was that I didn't. I didn't get married and have kids, buy a house or a car, or network and make new business contacts.

I refused to play along, and got left behind. Disconnected. Their conversations stopped making sense to me, nor did they interest me. I ceased to exist within their spheres. Heck, they didn't even notice that I was just sitting quietly for the past hour, as if invisible. And I was okay with that.

I stood up and left the room, apparently unnoticed. If they did notice, they probably thought I was heading to the bathroom. But I didn't go there. I kept walking, out onto the brightly lit streets.

The street was empty, except for the occasional taxi or car passing by. I looked at my watch; it was almost 1 am. The weather was pleasant and cool. The pavement was damp. Apparently, it had rained at some point in the past three hours while we were inside. But the clouds had already cleared, and I could see many stars twinkling against the red sky. Light pollution was heavy in this city so you could never see an absolutely black sky. Still, I could recognise some constellations. I crossed the street onto a walkway by the river to get a better view, but was annoyed at the persistent presence of street lamps everywhere, washing out the view of the stars. On a bridge nearby, I noticed one street lamp wasn't working, giving a small dark spot in the middle of the bridge. I stepped onto the bridge to see if I could get a clearer view of the sky.

I stood right under the broken lamp, the centre of the darkest spot on the bridge. I craned my neck to find Orion, the most easily recognisable constellation in the sky. Its features were so distinctive that I already knew this constellation as a kid long before knowing its name. It has three stars in the middle and a square of stars at its corners. During my undergraduate days, I had looked up the names of those three stars. Alnitak, Alnilam and Mintaka. That was Orion's belt. Somewhere around those three stars was a faint fuzz which was supposed to be the Orion Nebula, the birthplace of new stars.

I knew all those things because I was once interested in the cosmos, like any other kid. I remained interested long enough to choose physics as my major in university.

But I wasn't interested anymore.

My research for the PhD was mostly going nowhere. Even if I could finish, there were no job prospects other than teaching. Research was once new and exciting. Now it was a chore. I find myself doing what I have to, just to get through the day.

In a way, standing there, looking at Orion was a reunion similar to the reunion with David, 'Carltor' and Jessie. Orion was once a friend I was excited to meet all the time, but now it was a bore, like everything else. There was nothing to look forward to anymore.

My phone vibrated. It was probably them wondering where I was. I ignored it.

David was excited about a new career.

Carol and David had a new house, and were expecting a baby.

Jessie had a promising job and had just met a guy.

They had all played their cards right, taking the right chances and making the right decisions. Everything was on track. Even 'accidents' like an unexpected pregnancy couldn't derail them, they just moved sideways and settled onto a new track, always moving forward.

I stuck on one track and crashed.

What if all your mistakes piled up and you couldn't keep everything from falling apart? What if you fought entropy and lost? Well, what do you do when you lose a game and are not allowed to start over? Two options. Either fight back, or quit.

Quit the cosmic game.

'Are you going to jump?' said a voice that startled me. I turned around to find a man in a hoodie, hands in his pockets.

'Go away,' I said.

'Hey, man. I don't care if you jump or not. I was just wondering if you could leave your wallet behind. I mean, you ain't gonna need it anyway, right?'

'What makes you think I'm going to jump?'

'You have the look of a jumper. Standing on the bridge for an awful long time staring down. There ain't nothing down there but black.'

I looked down from the bridge. It was pitch black. He was right.

'Hmm,' I mumbled.

'Look man, I ain't here for a chat.'

'So get the fuck away.'

'I'm here to get your wallet.' He pulled out a knife from his jacket pocket, 'Just didn't want you to jump down with it.'

At first, I feared for my life. My blood started pumping, and I could feel my body starting to shake.

'Give it, now!'

'Okay, okay.' I reached for my wallet and pulled it out. As I did so, I happened to tilt my head towards the side of the bridge, looking at the blackness. He was right, I was just about to jump, so why was I scared of him? It didn't make sense.

No, it did make sense. Fear is a survival instinct, hard-coded into the brain. It's ironic how the higher, thinking functions of the brain are the ones that usually lead you onto a self-destructive path, not the older, primitive faculties — those keep you alive. Sometimes I wonder where evolution is heading.

'Throw it to me!' he demanded.

As I looked into the blackness, my fear receded. All the piled-up resentment morphed into anger. I turned to face him with a defiant eye.

'Fuck you,' I said, 'you're not getting my wallet.'

I tossed my wallet into the water. That pissed him off indeed. In one swift move, he stepped forward and stabbed me. I fell onto the pavement bleeding under the light of Orion.

Things fall apart in this game, especially if you start fighting back too late. Mistakes can pile up ... until it all blows up in your face.

———————

Meanwhile . . .

... in an Alternative Universe ...

As I looked into the blackness, my fear receded. Suddenly, the resentment of going to a reunion dinner with old friends became irrelevant. I looked at his face. Aside from the fact that he was threatening me with a knife, he looked very ordinary. Like any random person you walked by on the street.

Many people had walked past this guy and had never given him a second thought. But there is a story behind every face you see. I wondered what path in life had led him to this point, and realised with a start that I could easily have ended up in his shoes.

I had just spent the whole night with a group of people but had not truly listened to their stories, being busy judging them from my self-absorbed little world. I was the asshole all along.

He took the wallet and said, 'phone too'.

I gave him my phone, and he left without a word. It took a while for me to process what had just happened. I realised that I was shaking. It was the adrenaline rush. I did feel afraid for my life after all.

Eventually, I remembered my friends were still at the karaoke bar. For a moment, I considered bucking up, going back, and try to have a good time. But I didn't want to have to explain to them what just happened to me.

With no money or phone, all I could do was to walk home. Hopefully without being robbed again.

Jessie used to say that life is full of surprises. All you need to do was to hang on until a good one comes along.

Continue the adventures at
www.facebook.com/erebus.tenstories

About the Authors

May Han is a physics graduate who now prefers to spend time reading about and creating fictional worlds. She still likes physics and astronomy, but only as casual acquaintances, not as colleagues.

Yen Kheng is a physicist who works and teaches at the National University of Singapore.

Connect with the authors on Twitter
@LimYenKheng and @thongmayhan

Notes

Other titles published by SRI and SRI Books

Integrated Mathematics for Explorers

Solutions Manual: Integrated Mathematics for Explorers

Real World Mathematics

Solutions Manual: Real World Mathematics

Simplicity in Complexity: An Introduction to Complex Systems

Handbook of Mathematics

School Mathematics (Series)

Mathematical Escapades

Visit www.simplicitysg.net/books to view sample pages of the above books, explore purchasing options, and download some of our free E-books.